Salt Don't Go In Tea

J. Dominique

Salt Don't Go In Tea

Copyright © 2024 by J. Dominique

All rights reserved.

Published in the United States of America.

All rights reserved. No part of this publication may be reproduced, distributed, or transmitted in any form or by any means, including photocopying, recording, or other electronic or mechanical methods, without the prior written permission of the publisher, except in the case of brief quotations embodied in critical reviews and certain other noncommercial uses permitted by copyright law. For permission requests, please contact: www.colehartsignature.com

This is a work of fiction. Names, characters, places, and incidents either are the products of the author's imagination or are used fictitiously. Any resemblance of actual persons, living or dead, businesses, companies, events, or locales is entirely coincidental. The publisher does not have any control and does not assume any responsibility for author or third-party websites or their content.

The unauthorized reproduction or distribution of this copyrighted work is a crime punishable by law. No part of the book may be scanned, uploaded to or downloaded from file sharing sites, or distributed in any other way via the Internet or any other means, electronic, or print, without the publisher's permission. Criminal copyright infringement, including infringement without monetary gain, is investigated by the FBI and is punishable by up to five years in federal prison and a fine of $250,000 (www.fbi.gov/ipr/).

This book is licensed for your personal enjoyment only. Thank you for respecting the author's work.

Published by Cole Hart Signature, LLC.

Mailing List

To stay up to date on new releases, plus get information on contests, sneak peeks, and more,

Go To The Website Below...

www.colehartsignature.com

Amari

I let out a frustrated groan and set my phone back down. Once again, my baby daddy's stupid ass was ignoring my calls and texts when it was for something important. If I had been trying to give him some pussy he would have already been on his way over, but since it was for our son Prince, he was acting like he was too busy. Being an up-and-coming rapper often had him moving around and unavailable for Prince's day-to-day, and while I didn't like it, I handled my business without putting up a fuss. I only pressed him when I couldn't handle shit on my own, which wasn't very often, and every time, this was the result. Now I couldn't even focus on editing my video because I was too worried about the daycare bill looming over my head.

"Girl, why you over there huffing and puffing like that?" my bestie Koi asked, finally looking up from her phone. She'd been there for a half hour waiting for me to finish editing so I could do her makeup, and usually, I would've been done by now, but Malik's bullshit was distracting me.

"Malik's goofy ass." I rolled my eyes, not wanting to admit why I was so irritated, but I knew it was no point in trying to hide shit from her. Hearing his name instantly had her sucking her teeth as she prepared to hear the latest drama. "I told him

Wednesday that I was going to need the money for Prince's daycare bill by next week, and now he's not answering my calls."

She was already shaking her head before I even finished, and judging from the look on her face, she was about to give me an earful. "I don't know why you keep letting that man play in yo' face like that. Dola knows better than to fuck with me, I'll put his ass on child support so quick! Malik's lame ass only does that shit 'cause he knows you're not gonna do nothin' but complain for a little while and then act like ain't shit happened!" Her voice grew high pitched the more she spoke, and I lifted a perfectly arched brow at her. It was well known that Koi didn't like Malik, and according to her, she never had. Back when her baby daddy Dola had introduced us, I thought it would be cute for us to be best friends and also date rappers that were friends. At twenty-one, the thought of turning up in clubs and going on tour together with our niggas seemed cool as hell, but fast forward five years later, and I was realizing just how stupid I'd been. For some reason, I never thought about the groupies or the late nights in the studio when I was having my fantasies about a future with Malik. I was in love and convinced that he loved me enough that none of those things would be an issue, but they ended up being the biggest reasons we didn't last. Not only had Malik cheated on me multiple times, but throughout my entire pregnancy, he'd been too busy in the studio or at a show to be actively involved. He couldn't even put the rap shit on the back burner the night I went into labor with Prince. Because of his image, only the people closest to him even knew about me and our son's existence, but I'd let all that slide. The final straw, though, was him choosing to stay on the road instead of bringing his dumb ass home when I'd lost our second baby. If it wasn't obvious before, it became crystal clear then that he didn't give a shit about me, not over his career anyway, but I still hoped he would step up as far as Prince was concerned. Evidently, I hadn't learned my lesson.

"I bet if you put his clown ass on child support he wouldn't be ignoring your calls! It's the least he could do to pay for daycare considering that he ain't here to watch him!"

Koi was still ranting when I tuned back into the conversation, and I immediately shook my head. As much as I despised Malik, the last thing I wanted to do was force him to provide for our son. It should've been something that came naturally to him, just like it had to me. Plus, I feared that taking him to court would only push him further away and out of Prince's life.

"I'm not doing that. I don't want to make him take care of his responsibilities. I'd rather he do it on his own," I explained, realizing just how stupid I sounded as soon as the words left my mouth.

"Bitch, you sound dumb as hell! He has the option to do it on his own now but he's dodging yo' ass like you're a groupie!" Koi turned her nose up and shook her head. "You're a better one than me, I'll tell you that much."

"Well we can't all have a baby daddy that actually does what he's supposed to," I said smartly. Koi really didn't know how good she had it, despite the shit she talked. Since I'd known Dola he had always made sure that she and their daughter Blaze were good. He was the epitome of a good man even when Koi was giving him her ass to kiss, and because of him, she was able to monetize their connection. My girl had gone from hosting club events to being a brand ambassador, and the more she rose in the ranks, the more she rubbed shoulders with the elite. They'd been broken up for years now, and since then, she'd been linked to more than a few get-money niggas, which was another reason she didn't get along with Malik. He thought she was a hoe, and that if I hung out with her I'd be seen as one too, but I was starting to think it was really because he thought she'd introduce me to somebody better.

"Shit, even if my baby daddy didn't do what he was supposed to, I'd still find another nigga that would. That's yo' problem now, you're way too worried about Malik's ass and he don't give a fuck about you. Matter fact, why don't you come out with me?

This new dude I'm talkin' to got heavy pockets and I know the niggas he hangs with got money too." Her eyes gleamed with excitement as she spoke, probably thinking what she'd said would excite me too, but that was the furthest thing from the truth. I was too deep in my bag to be trying to entertain any niggas. Malik was enough and I wasn't even with his ass.

"Hell no! I still need to finish this video and figure out how I'm gone get this money before Monday."

"Bitch, that shit can wait, and I'll even pay for Prince's daycare just to get you out the house and around some niggas with money," she offered with raised brows. Any argument I had died on my tongue. As bad as I wanted to decline, it was already Saturday, and no matter how much I hustled, I knew I wasn't going to be able to come up with the almost five-hundred-dollar bill by Monday. The last thing I wanted was to have to ask my mama for help again. She was already picking up Malik's slack, and I didn't want to burden her any more than I already was. "Come on girl, it ain't like you got anything better to do." Koi continued pushing as I weighed the pros and cons of going out with her in my head.

"Okay, okay, fine, but I'm not talkin' to nobody so don't be tryna play matchmaker," I warned, narrowing my eyes at her while she squealed happily. Unfazed, she jumped up to find me something to wear, and all I could do was pray she didn't get me into some bullshit.

AMARI

The entire ride to the club I had to listen to Koi brag about her mystery man and how much money she'd been getting from him. I'd never been attracted to a nigga solely based on his funds, so I wasn't impressed by the shit she was telling me, but with what I had going on with my baby daddy, I was beginning to rethink my stance. Koi was out here with a baby daddy that did his job and niggas to pick up his slack while I was being bribed into a night at the club with daycare money. The shit was really tragic and had me even more irritated.

"Ugh, we really should've stopped by my house and got you another dress," Koi complained while checking her makeup. This was the third time she'd complained about my outfit since we got in the car, and I couldn't help rolling my eyes. "These niggas really touching money and if you hang around them, you need to look the part. What if one of them wanna kick it with you but realize yo' ass wearing that SHEIN original?"

"Girl, fuck you and them niggas! I was just supposed to be tagging along anyway, so what I got on shouldn't concern any of y'all."

Koi's eyes stretched wide and she dismissively sucked her teeth. "It really ain't that serious, Amari. I was just sayin', but if you don't want a nigga with money then I'll leave it alone." She threw her hands up and shrugged like she hadn't just insulted me. It took everything in me to not just say fuck it and go home, but with Malik still playing hide and seek, staying was my only option. That didn't mean I couldn't pretend like I wouldn't though.

"Please do, 'cause I have no problem taking my ass back home." I pinned her with a look just as we stopped in front of the club. Without giving her a chance to respond, I climbed out and adjusted my skirt while I waited for her to join me on the sidewalk.

Catcalls erupted as soon as she did, but just like me, she ignored them. For Koi, it was because none of them had enough pull to not be standing in that long ass line while I just wasn't trying to be bothered. Honestly, after all the shit she'd talked, I was more interested in finally finding out who her mystery man was anyway.

We bypassed the line and quickly made it through security, which wasn't a surprise since Koi was so well known. It was packed body to body inside and I had to hold on to Koi's arm to make sure I didn't lose her as she snaked her way through the crowd. Before I knew it, we were entering one of the VIP sections that, thankfully, wasn't as packed. It even provided privacy screens so nobody could see inside but we could see out. Koi instantly headed toward the huge sectional in the middle of the room where only three men sat, and I narrowed my eyes.

The flashing lights made it hard to see their faces, but the closer we got I was able to recognize Saint Savage. Seeing him had me looking around for his fiancée Yara. They were the IT couple, with Saint being the president of Savage Records and Yara being a social media influencer and model. I'd been working myself up to get on her level with my YouTube channel and I couldn't help getting excited about the opportunity to pick her brain. I was so busy looking for Yara that I was no longer paying attention to Koi. That was until I did another sweep of the room to see her wrapped around Saint like he wasn't in a very public relationship!

I just knew damn well she hadn't dragged me along for her hoetivities!

I watched them in disbelief, too shook to even move because I just had to be seeing shit. There was no way the nigga Koi had been bragging about this whole time was Saint Savage, but if I had any doubt, her kissing him cleared that shit right up. By now, I was standing right next to them and I promptly cleared my throat.

"Oh, my bad girl, this is my boo, Saint. Saint, this is my bestie, Amari!" she gushed all too happily, like this wasn't an awkward situation. Judging by the look on his face, Saint wasn't aware of me tagging along, and he wasn't comfortable with it either. He hit me with a dry 'sup' and a head nod, avoiding my eyes.

"Hey." I gave him the same energy and turned my attention back to Koi. I didn't bother trying to mask my judgment either because I definitely wanted her ass to see it.

"Weeeeellll, come make us a drink, babe." Koi tilted her head up at Saint, ignoring the daggers I was shooting her way. The sugary sweet tone she'd used was one I'd never heard from her. She damn sure didn't even sound like the same woman that was in the car talking about how heavy this nigga's wallet was. I trailed after them as she pulled him back over to the couch where the two other guys were still sitting. One of them held a bottle in each hand as he bopped along to the loud music while the other leaned forward, lighting a blunt. He was sexy as hell, and the mean mug on his face made him look even better.

Saint dropped onto the far end of the couch and pulled Koi along with him before mixing her up a drink. Rude ass didn't even do introductions. I guess I could understand why, but little did he know I had no intentions of ever being around any of them again. I took it upon myself to find my own seat, which happened to be the only one left and was right next to the handsome brooder. As if only just noticing me, he looked over with the same annoyed expression and raised his thick brows. Instead of voicing his dissatisfaction, he shifted so that he was closer to the nigga with the bottles. I quickly surmised that all of these niggas were rude as hell.

"Daaaamn! Where the fuck yo' fine ass come from?"

I rolled my eyes and grabbed one of the many bottles of Patrón from the table. Usually, I liked having a chaser with my drinks, but I was going to need straight shots to make it through a couple hours with these niggas. Ignoring him, I pulled my phone back out and checked for a message or call from Malik...again, and again, there was nothing.

"Nah, for real, what's up with you? I'm Flex, and this antisocial ass nigga is Psalm. What's yo' name?" he continued even though I hadn't given him any reason to think I wanted to have a conversation with his ass. It was just like a nigga not to take a hint. Next, he'd be cursing me out once he realized I wasn't giving him any play.

"That's my girl Amari!"

I shot Koi a look that could kill, only for her to grin widely and shrug. She'd been so busy sucking Saint's face that I didn't think she was paying us any mind, but clearly, she was, and clearly, she was still trying to play Cupid.

"Ooh, *Amari*, I like that." Flex leered at me, making sure I saw the diamond grill in his mouth. He must've been used to women falling at his feet whenever he opened his mouth because he hadn't closed that shit since he noticed me. Thankfully, Psalm was sitting between us or I was sure he'd have tried to touch me by now. I gave him a phony smile and hoped it didn't look too much like a grimace before draining my glass and reaching to pour another.

"What the fuck!" Koi shrieked as Saint jumped up frantically, damn near making her fall. Embarrassment covered her face but he didn't seem to care, rushing off with his phone to his ear. Nobody else even flinched, like they were used to this behavior, but I rushed to her side.

"Damn bitch, you okay?" I touched her arm since she was so busy staring after Saint that she didn't notice or give a damn that I was right there. "What the fuck wrong with that nigga?" I followed her line of sight to where he was now walking back.

"Look, my girl comin' up here, y'all gotta go," he huffed, making her jaw drop.

"Saint, this is supposed to be our night!" Koi looked like she was near tears as she grabbed ahold of his shirt, and even I had to give her a side eye. He gripped her hands up in his, removing them with a little push.

"Yo' ass deaf or somethin'?" he spat as his phone lit up and panic covered his face. "Fuck! Fuck! Sit yo' ass down next to Flex and play along." Without waiting for her to do what he said, he walked off, smoothing out his clothes.

Koi glared at his back for a few seconds before turning like she was really about to listen to him, and I yanked her back. I could see the irritation all in her face, but I wasn't sure if it was for me or the nigga that had her playing the side. "Bitch, what you doin'? Let's go."

"No, *we're* going to sit down like Saint said." She snatched away and took a seat next to Flex, nodding for me to do the same. I couldn't imagine Saint's ass was giving her enough money to look this stupid, but here she was. The queen of stupidity. Shaking my head, I went back to where I was sitting next to Psalm.

"Ayee, look who decided to come crash the party," Psalm spoke for the first time and gave a genuine smile when Saint walked up with Yara and her friend Jasmin. Just from the little bit of time I'd spent around him, I knew I didn't like Saint's ass, and I absolutely hated the shit he had going on with Koi, but I couldn't help being geeked about Yara's presence. She was just as cute in real life as she was online, and she looked amazing in the white feather dress she was wearing.

"Nigga please, I am the party," Yara quipped, flipping her braids over her shoulder.

"Yeah, till SJ call and tell yo' ass to come home!" The mention of her and Saint's son had her eyes rolling despite the proud smile she wore.

"Not tonight he ain't. He's with y'all mama and he knows Grandma Angel don't play that phone shit after bedtime." She snaked her neck at him, and I shot a surprised look his way. *He was Saint's brother?* The entire time I'd been there, I hadn't noticed their resemblance, but now it was unmistakable. I wondered why I'd never heard of or seen him before but then again, I wasn't into the rap scene like that. I only knew Saint because of his appearances with Yara so it made sense that Psalm wasn't on my radar.

"Yeah ayite, don't let her ass fool you. He probably blowing up yo' shit right now while she laid up watching reruns and shit."

"Anyway, you're so busy talkin' shit you didn't even introduce me." She dismissed him with a wave and her eyes bounced between us encouragingly. I felt the exact moment his body stiffened, even though he'd moved over as much as he could. Besides Saint directing Koi's silly ass to sit next to Flex, he hadn't really said shit to the rest of us, and Yara assuming that I was with him had caught us both off guard. Before I could speak though, he shrugged coolly and nodded my way.

"This is Amari," he said, letting out a thick cloud of smoke through his nose.

"Ugh, I swear you're so annoying." Yara sucked her teeth. "Amari? That's really pretty. I'm Yara, this meanie's future sister-in-law. It's nice to meet you."

"I knew I recognized you. You got that YouTube channel Amari's Beats?" Jasmin spoke up for the first time, and I couldn't help beaming. It wasn't often that I was recognized, so for Yara's best friend to know who I was had me stunned.

"Uhh, yeah, that's me."

"Oooh, I knew it! I watch your videos all the time! I can't do my own hair or makeup, but I love watching you and imagining that I can." She laughed. "You make it look so easy."

"Aww, thank you! It definitely took some time to teach

myself, but after a while, everything got easier," I admitted with a shrug. I'd always had a flare for anything beauty, so it wasn't hard to get into hair and makeup, but learning how to do the latest trends on myself had taken a lot of time. Once I got it down though, it was nothing, and I was becoming a beast in my own right.

"You do hair and makeup?"

"Yeah girl, remember I showed you the video of her doing that 360 on herself," Jasmin reminded, and Yara's eyes bulged.

"That's you?" she quizzed, and I nodded sheepishly. "Oh, I'm gonna have to get up with you. Maybe we can collab or something?" The offer had everybody tuned in, and I was suddenly uncomfortable with all the attention being on me. As excited as Yara seemed, I could feel Koi burning a hole in the side of my face right along with Saint. It was obvious neither of them were feeling the conversation, but like I said, linking up with Yara was a dream and I wasn't going to pass it up just because Koi was on some hoe shit.

"Just let me know when and where." I was acting smooth on the outside, but inside I was jumping for joy at the possibility. If I got Yara on my channel or if I made an appearance on hers, that was going to be big for me. I could already imagine the types of doors it would open, and I immediately felt thankful that I'd decided to come.

PSALM

"Yoooo, what the fuck you doin', boy?"

I quickly blacked out my phone screen as my brother's loud ass entered the studio with the same hoe from the other night. I was in the middle of a break, and the last thing I wanted to do was entertain him and his groupie, but he ignored the look on my face and pulled her onto the couch with him. I'd been preaching to his goofy ass for months about tightening up, but he obviously wasn't heeding my warnings. Every time I turned around, he was popping up with shorty on his arm like Yara wouldn't leave him if she caught wind of this. Real shit, he'd gotten lucky the other night, but if he kept fucking around, he was going to lose his girl behind a money-hungry hoe.

"Nah, what the fuck is you doin'? I know you supposed to be the big brother, but yo' ass acting like a lil' nigga. Fuck you keep bringing this broad around for?" I mugged her, irritated by the ditzy look on her face.

"Uh, scuse you!"

"Bitch, you're excused," I shot back, daring her to say something. She was lucky I didn't want to see Yara hurt, or I'd tell my sis just so I could see her get her ass beat.

"Damn bro, chill." Saint's interjection was weak as fuck, and probably only for appearance's sake, because he knew damn well neither of us gave a fuck about that hoe's feelings. That shit made what he was doing even more annoying for me. His ass was jeopardizing his family for a bitch he didn't even really give a fuck about, and I was starting to think she was giving him drugs or something.

"Tell her ass don't say shit to me then."

"Don't talk about me like I ain't right here!" Koi sucked her teeth.

"Get the fuck out then you won't be right here."

"Babe!" she gasped like Saint was going to stop me from saying what the fuck I wanted, but all he did was run a hand down his face.

"Just wait for me in my office, ma," he sighed, and she stomped out of the room, pissed. "Man, why the fuck you keep comin' at her like that?" he asked once she'd slammed the door behind her, and I snorted.

"Fuck that groupie bitch. You gone keep playin' and Yara gone leave yo' goofy ass." I lit the blunt I'd been holding onto this entire time, taking a deep pull since he had come in and fucked up my vibe.

"I wish you'd stop sayin' that shit, nigga. Yara ain't goin' nowhere. Stop wishing that evil on me with yo' hatin' ass," he grumbled with his face all balled up, and I shrugged.

"Keep thinkin' that shit," I warned, blowing out a stream of smoke as I leaned back in my chair. He could keep fucking around if he wanted to, but when Yara packed up her and the kids, I was gone be the main one helping her carry her boxes out.

"Whatever muhfucka, I ain't come down here to listen to you talk shit. I came 'cause I want you to check out this new artist. He's a rapper, and from what I've seen he's got a lot of raw talent." He quickly changed the subject, knowing I'd focus on business if he brought it up. I definitely trusted him when it came to talent, even if I didn't trust his judgment on other shit. I stroked my chin as I listened to him run down the nigga's stats, already pulling up a video to show me. "His name is Malice. Right now, he's still underground, but the word is he's looking for a label." I couldn't lie, the small clip he showed me was pretty good. He had the look down, and his delivery was decent, although from what I could see, he needed to work on his stage presence.

"He write his own shit?" I wanted to know, not that it mattered because there were plenty of artists out that had writers and people orchestrating their whole image. If he was as good as he seemed, we'd find somebody to write his rhymes for him.

"I think so." He shrugged. "He's got a show coming up, though; we can go check him out."

"That's cool." I took another pull of my blunt and handed him his phone back. "Leave yo' cum dump at home tho'."

"Fuck outta here." He laughed at the warning, but I was dead ass serious. He was starting to get too comfortable and that shit was rubbing me the wrong way. I wasn't the most perfect nigga, but I hadn't ever blatantly disrespected my baby mama the way Saint was doing. Shit, me and Unique hadn't been together in over a year, and I still wouldn't do half the shit he'd done. "You talkin' shit, but if she fuck around and bring Amari with her, yo' ass ain't gone be complaining."

"Yeah, ayite." I tossed his phone back to him with a shake of my head. I could admit that Amari was bad as fuck, but despite thinking she was nice to look at, I didn't have shit for her, especially if she was hanging around with a bitch like Koi. It had been my experience that birds of a feather flocked together, and although I hadn't heard shit about Amari or seen her around, it was safe to assume she got down like her girl. Saint was still grinning at me like a fool, unfazed by my weak dismissal, but I wasn't going to give his cheating ass the satisfaction of being even partly right. "Get yo' ugly ass out my session," I grimaced, spinning around so my back was to him, but he only laughed as I began pressing shit on the soundboard. Thankfully, he took his funny-looking ass on somewhere and left me alone just as our artist Raylin returned.

A couple of hours later, I was finished with the track we'd been working on and I was alone once again. I lifted my phone and Amari's face was the first thing I saw, reminding me of the stalking I'd been doing before Saint brought his goofy ass in. I'd gone from flipping through her videos with a mixture of disgust and ardor to talking shit about her, but it was like I couldn't stop myself. It bothered me that I liked her far beyond her physical appearance. Despite the things I'd said, she didn't seem like that bitch Koi at all, but looks could be deceiving, and I wasn't trying to take any chances. With that thought in mind, I quickly closed out of YouTube and checked my messages. The first one was from Saint's annoying ass, then a couple from Unique, and the last one was from my OG. I hit my mama back first, and she picked up on the first ring like she was waiting on me.

"What's up, Ma?"

"Boy, don't what's up me! Unique been blowing up my phone and leaving messages looking for you, and it seems like your phone works just fine!" The smile I'd been wearing instantly fell, and I ran a hand down my face with a sigh. I hadn't opened any of Unique's messages, so I didn't know what she wanted, but it had to be something serious if she was hitting up my mama.

"Shit, what her ass want? I ain't talked to Unique in a minute," I admitted. In the time that we'd been apart, I hadn't gone out of my way to talk to her and neither had she, which made her suddenly popping up random as hell.

"Well, I think you need to find out, then call me back." Her rude ass hung up on me, and I couldn't do shit but laugh. Leave it to my OG to be forcing a nigga to act right. If she knew about the shit Saint was out here doing, she would've already beat him and Koi's ass, but I wasn't a snitch so she'd have to find that out on her own. I just hoped I was there when she did because I wanted to record that beat down.

Stretching my legs out in front of me, I dialed Unique's number and tried to prepare myself for whatever her ass wanted. It had been a couple months since she'd hit my line for anything, so I didn't know what to expect. Even though she'd just texted not even an hour before, her phone went to voicemail both times I tried to call. Just as I was about to say fuck it, my phone went off in my hand and I quickly pressed accept.

"What type of fuckin' games yo' ass playin', Nique? This shit ain't phone tag—"

"Where the fuck have you been?" she shouted, cutting me off, and my face instantly tightened. "I've been calling and texting you all day and you haven't answered not once!"

"Fuck is you yellin' at?" I sat up, irritated. She knew better than anybody that I didn't respond well to all that extra shit. She was lucky that I'd even called her ass back, but she was going to have to pipe down if she wanted me to stay on the phone.

"You, nigga! I'm yellin' at yo' weak ass!" she went on, ignoring the warning in my tone. "You don't even know what today is and you got the nerve to have an attitude with me! Fuck you, Psalm!" Her ass hung up, leaving me even more pissed and confused, until I thought about what she'd said. There could've only been one day that had her calling me all hysterical and shit, except there was no way I'd tweaked and forgotten. A quick look at my phone screen confirmed that I had though. *August 6th*.

I instantly felt like shit. In the five years since me and Unique had lost our son, I'd never forgotten the day he'd died. Then again, this was the first year we hadn't been together on this day. Unique had always been a reminder of what we'd lost, even without having to actually remind me. Our crib together was full of mementos. Everything from his first ultrasound picture to his last. Unique still had clothes, blankets, stuffed animals, and all types of shit that made it hard to forget about him. It had been hard to convince her to part with any of his things, and if I had left it up to her, she'd have kept his entire bedroom intact. Me not wanting to stay buried under his memory was the main reason we'd broken up. I couldn't keep living under the grief of our loss, and I didn't think my presence was helping her out of it. I'd tried to get her to talk to someone, but she'd refused, and after a while, I'd assumed that she was doing better. This phone call proved otherwise though.

"Fuck!" I cursed as guilt ate away at me. I'd tried so hard to move past his death that I'd basically left Unique to fend for herself. Snatching up my keys, I rushed out, hoping she was home.

When I pulled up to our old apartment, I paused before using my key to let myself in. I didn't know what to expect on the other side of the door and I tried to brace myself. "Unique!" I called out when I didn't find her in the living room or kitchen. Really, I'd been hoping not to have to go into his bedroom despite knowing that's where she'd probably be, and when she yelled back, it was confirmed.

"Get out!"

I stopped at our son's room to find Unique lying in the middle of the floor, holding the teddy bear that had his heartbeat recorded on it in one hand and a liter of Tito's in the other. Sighing, I leaned against the doorframe and took her in. Despite her hair being all over her head and her face being swollen from crying, she was still beautiful.

Her nose turned up and she tossed one of her flip flops at my head, missing by inches. "I said get out!" she repeated, glaring at me with those hazel eyes I used to love so much.

"I fucked up, I know that, Nique. Shit just been hectic lately, and it slipped my mind—"

She cut me off with a maniacal laugh. "It slipped your *mind*! Our fuckin' baby's birthday slipped your mind?"

"Yes, Nique, shit. I forgot! Between the artists we already signed and the new ones we're looking into, he slipped my mind, but I'm here now!"

"Nigga please!" she scoffed, taking another sip of her drink. "You can't even say his name! Be honest with yourself! You forgot Legend 'cause you don't give a fuck! You never did! Probably wanted me to get an abortion—"

"Aye, don't say no shit like that. I wanted him. Shit, I *still* want him! Don't ever say no shit like that, Nique."

"Tuh! You can't even say his name." Her voice quivered with the accusation, and as bad as I wanted to deny it, I couldn't. I'd avoided saying his name because it made the shit hurt less, it made it easier to cope, and while it wasn't the best way to handle the shit, I was able to make it through the day. My silence only encouraged her to keep going and I just shoved my hands in my pockets with a sigh. "All this time I've been blaming myself, thinking that maybe I did something wrong, when it was yo' weak ass stressing me out. You think I didn't know about them hoes you was messing with and that bitch Free, hmm? I knew about all that shit and I never said nothing because I just wanted you and I ended up losing my baby! You was out fuckin' that hoe while I was losing our baby, and you still ain't even apologized for that shit!"

She caught me by surprise with that one. Free was one of the first artists I'd worked with, and long nights in the studio had quickly turned into weed-induced fuck sessions that became like an addiction for me. We had a connection through our music, the type that had me pushing my girl away and falling deeper into whatever the fuck I thought I had with her. That's how I'd ended up with her on the night that Unique went into the hospital after waking up in a blood-soaked bed. The bitch had silenced my phone, so by the time I saw all the missed calls and made my way to the hospital, I was too late. That guilt ate at me and had me ready to kill Free's goofy ass, but shit, I was to blame too. I'd allowed that shit to happen because if I'd been my ass at home where I was supposed to be, shit probably would've went different. How and when Unique found out some shit I hadn't even told my brother was beyond me, but it brought back that crushing weight I'd been trying hard to get away from. I couldn't even bring myself to deny it. I ran my hand down my face and searched for the right words even though there were none.

"Just go, Psalm," Unique said lowly, sucking her teeth when I still didn't make a move to leave. "GET THE FUCK OUT!" she shrieked when I still hadn't moved, and I took that as my cue to go. I'd fucked up enough for one night, and my presence only seemed to be making shit worse for her. One thing my visit had encouraged me to do, though, was find the nearest bottle and drown myself in that shit.

Amari

"I don't think you should do it."

I rolled my eyes and tossed more things in my bag as Koi whined in the phone. It had been almost two weeks since the night I went out with her, and Yara had finally gotten with me about doing her hair. Although it was extremely short notice, I still jumped at the chance, and Koi had been trying to convince me not to go for the last ten minutes.

"You sound crazy as hell. For one, I already told her I was coming, and for two, Yara being on my channel is big! I can't pass that up." I frowned, trying to resist the urge to curse her out. I'd already had to tell her about herself after she'd thrown me into her messy ass situation at the club and she barely apologized for that. In her mind I was the one in the wrong for even being friendly with Yara, despite neither of us having a reason to dislike her. Koi was fucking her man and acting as if Yara had done her wrong. I could never understand side bitch logic, and I never wanted any dick that would have me that delusional.

"Whatever, you've been doin' my hair and makeup for years and you never wanted to put me on your channel," she complained, and my jaw dropped at the lie. I'd asked her to let me use her for content multiple times, but she'd always had an excuse, especially once she started blowing up. After she told me it wouldn't be a good look because of a contract she had with another hairstylist, I let it go and never asked again. Just like with Malik, I didn't want to fuck up her potential money, but it always rubbed me the wrong way that neither of them were willing to put me on. Now that I had another means though, she wanted to complain and try to stand in the way of my bag.

"You're a damn lie! I asked you before I even asked my mama!" I stood up straight with my hand on my hip like she could see me even though I was across the room. There was no way she was being serious, but her ass definitely was.

"I mean, that was a long time ago, though." I could hear the pout in her voice, and I waved her off.

"Yeah, 'cause you told me you signed some contract with Tina Jay," I reminded her, and the line went silent for a beat.

"Oh...well, I been out of that, so you can use me as your model and cancel with Yara. I'm bigger than her anyway. You'll get way more views with me." It was my turn to go quiet. She'd definitely just lied through her teeth with that one, but I wasn't the type of friend that would bust her bubble. If she thought she was a bigger presence than Yara, I'd let her have that. I was actually thankful when her daughter Blaze came up and distracted her. "Not now, Blaze! Don't you see me on the phone? Go ask Mama!"

I rolled my eyes at how quickly she'd dismissed her baby to go to her mom when she already barely had her. With my work schedule and side hustle taking up so much of my time, I always cherished any moment I had with Prince, but that was the difference between me and Koi. She'd had her baby to try and keep Dola, but since they weren't together she was no longer interested in her. I was already tired of being on the phone with her at this point. "I gotta go, my ride is here. I'll call you when I get back," I lied quickly and hung up before she could try and keep me on the phone any longer. With her out of my ear, my music resumed, and the vibe I had going on before she'd called returned as I finished packing up my bag. I sang along to SZA and double checked that I had everything I needed before heading out since my Uber was only a few minutes away.

As I walked down to the front porch, I texted Yara to let her know I would be on my way. The heat hit me hard as hell and I instantly regretted coming down so soon when my ride wasn't going to be there for a few. I used my hand to fan myself and squinted when I saw my mama's car slowly pulling into the lone parking spot in front of my building. She was supposed to be watching Prince for me while I was at Yara's, so to see her here now, my heart dropped to my stomach.

"Good, I caught you. My phone died before I could call, but I forgot I'm on call since that bitch Lisa likes to call off so much," she huffed as she rushed around the car fully dressed in her scrubs and Crocs. By the time I came down the steps, she already had Prince out of his seat and was meeting me on the curb.

"Ma—"

"Don't ma me, girl! What part of on-call don't you understand!" she cut me off before I could start my complaint. "I'll come pick him back up tomorrow, and we can go to the zoo."

"Yaaaaay! Hey Mommy!" He sounded chipper, stuffing his mouth with the apple slices that came with his Happy Meal.

"Hey baby." I tried not to sound disappointed even though I was torn between canceling or just bringing him with me. I rubbed the top of his head as my mama gave him a quick kiss.

"Bye, granny's baby, I'll see you tomorrow!" She was already back on the driver's side as he shouted out goodbye and tried to wave even though his hands were full. Sighing, I hoisted my bag more securely on my shoulder just as my Uber pulled into the spot my mama had just left. As unprofessional as it was to bring Prince with me, I felt like it was too late to cancel, so I ushered him over to the car while he ran down everything he'd done while with his grandma.

By the time we reached Yara and Saint's big ass house, I was nervous and regretting my decision. I'd seen her interior before in the background of her videos and lives, but pulling up to the pristine-looking house had me wondering if I could keep Prince from showing his ass. He was usually very well behaved, but he'd also never had so much space to play in, and that had me second guessing myself.

"Hey, we're here!" the driver snapped irritably since I hadn't made a move to get out yet. I shot him an annoyed look in the rearview, before gathering Prince's mess and my bag. His mouth was still going a mile a minute as we struggled up to the door, and I hit the Ring doorbell with my elbow. I could hear her and the kids inside, and they were right on her heels as she opened the door with a flustered grin. She'd taken down her braids and had her long hair freshly washed and blown out like I'd requested.

"Hey girl! I'm glad you could make it!" she gushed, and her eyes fell on Prince at my side. "Awww, and you brought somebody to play! I didn't know you had a baby, he's so cute!"

I couldn't help smiling at the compliment as she lifted her little girl, Coco, up onto her hip. "Yeah, I'm sorry about that...my sitter canceled last minute and—" She cut me off with a wave and moved back so we could come in.

"It happens to the best of us. You don't know how many times I've had to drag them along because Saint was busy and I didn't have a backup." Relief flooded me as I entered the foyer with a suddenly shy Prince gripping my leg tightly. I loved that she was just as down to earth in real life as she was online. She didn't have a nanny and was very active in her kids' life, just like me. Clad in a pair of Savage Fenty biker shorts and the matching sports bra, she didn't even look like she'd had a baby six months ago as she padded off barefoot, leading me further inside. "Do you want anything? I got pop, juice, water," she offered while I took in how nice her house was. Usually, her videos were limited to certain rooms or areas so to see it all together had me in awe.

"No thank you." I followed her into the large kitchen, where she grabbed a few snacks for the kids, and I tossed Prince's trash away, nodding when she mouthed if he could have one. As soon as he peeped the package of fruit snacks in her hands, his little phony ass let me go and ran around the island just like SJ did.

"Okay Saint, we're about to go in my beauty room, take..." she paused, waiting for me to fill in the gap.

"Prince."

"Oooh, that's cute! Take Prince in the playroom, and be careful with those fruit snacks! I don't wanna find none in there on the floor!" she yelled at his back as they ran off together. Rolling her eyes, she turned back to me. "They'll be right next to the room we're in," she let me know, now prepping a bottle for the baby with ease. As I watched her talk to Coco, I couldn't help wondering if I would've had a girl the second time around. I tried not to think too much about the baby I'd lost because it was so early on and shit in my life was so bad then, but seeing Yara with her little girl had my heart hurting for what I'd lost. She'd barely finished shaking the formula up before Coco snatched it away and began guzzling it down, making us both laugh.

"Somebody's hungry."

"Yeah, she's a greedy little thing, and Saint and his mama don't make it no better letting her taste everything she sees." She shook her head as Coco laid down on her shoulder. "She's about ready for a nap, though, so she'll be out in a few. Come on." Yara switched off, and we ended up in her glam room. She laid the baby in the playpen that was in the corner and I started setting up at her vanity. The wig she wanted installed was already prepped and sitting on top of a mannequin head. Right away, I could see that the hair was luscious and colored to perfection. It was from a hair company called Simply Hair, and I'd ordered a wig or two from them myself with the same results. I still had mine, and it had been months since I'd installed them, but they still looked good.

"Okay, I'm ready." Yara came over and dropped into her pink swivel chair after setting up her phone on the tripod. "You ready, girl?" She looked up at me, finger poised over the live button as I finished setting my things on her vanity. I'd been so busy getting set up that I hadn't had time to think about how many people were about to be viewing me. Every time Yara went live, there were a few thousand people who joined, and I wanted to make sure I didn't fuck up in real time. Taking a deep breath, I nodded and Yara gave me a reassuring smile.

"Yeah, I think so."

"Listen, you got this. I've seen your work so I know you're gonna lay the shit out this wig," she encouraged, winking at me as the live connected and she immediately went into influencer mode. "Hey y'all! It's that time again. As y'all can see, I've taken down my braids so I gotta get something done to this head. Chill with me while I get my hair laid and slayed by my girl Amari, and make sure y'all tune in to her YouTube channel, Amari Beats, 'cause she does it all! Everything from hair to makeup and even nails! Yeah, she's a whole triple threat out here! Say hey, girl!"

"Heyyyy! If you're tuning in from my channel, drop some hearts in the chat!" I said, unable to keep the tremor out of my voice, but seeing a flood of pink hearts popping up had me feeling more at ease. I silently pumped myself up, remembering that I did this all the time. Yara cut on some music as she continued answering questions while I started the process of braiding her hair down and answering a few that were directed to me. Between the music and the flow of the conversation, I got into a groove and forgot all about my nerves. It didn't take long to have her hair braided and tucked underneath a wig cap, and we took a short break to check on the kids before continuing.

Before I knew it, we were finished and I stood back admiring my work. I'd added a loose curl and swooped her baby hairs to perfection, and as she turned from side to side showing it off, I patted myself on the back. People were already asking about booking me in the comments and I let them know they could hit me up on my socials before Yara ended the live.

"See, I knew you'd kill that shit!" she hyped me up as soon as it closed out.

"You were definitely right. Thanks so much for this. My

phones are already blowing up with new subscribers and friend requests." I grabbed my phone off the stand and ended the recording, unable to stop myself from smiling hard at each of the notifications that were coming in. It seemed like almost everybody who'd been on Yara's live had come to my page and subscribed to my YouTube. It was exhilarating and had me pumped up.

"Duh girl, I'm always right," she joked, tossing her hair. "But now since we got the business stuff out the way. What's up with you and my brother? Y'all got a date planned yet?"

I was lost for all of five seconds before I remembered being thrown together with Psalm a couple weeks ago. Involuntarily, my face balled up at the memory, and she took that as my answer, letting out a giggle.

"That nigga." She shook her head. "How he mess up already?"

Besides what we'd let her assume at the club, I didn't know what he'd told her about us. I figured if anything, his mean ass hadn't said shit, which left me with the task of making up some type of excuse. At least with her putting the blame on him, it made things easier. "No offense, but he's an asshole." My eyes rolled up into my head and Yara nodded in understanding.

"I've heard that a few times," she admitted with a sigh. "He, uh, he's been through some stuff in the last few years and it made him a little...guarded. It might come off as being an asshole, but I promise he's really not that bad once you give him a chance."

"Uhhh, I think that ship has sailed, boo," I said, sending us both into a fit of cackles.

"Okay, okay, I'll leave it alone. I just don't want it to be awkward 'cause you're cool as hell, and after the way you just whipped this hair, I'ma have to keep you a—" She stopped midsentence as the front door alerted us that someone had entered.

"Yooo! Where y'all niggas at!" I cringed hearing Psalm's voice and Yara started snickering, that was until the baby woke up screaming.

"God dammit!" Grabbing one of the clips I'd been using, she

put her hair up and rushed over to Coco just as Psalm came in. For as rude as he was, I couldn't lie and say his ass wasn't fine as hell. Even in just a black t-shirt, Nike track pants, and some slides, he was giving straight sex appeal. His dick print was evident and I instantly wondered how much bigger it was when he was actually hard. I shook off my lustful thoughts and focused on putting my things away before he could catch me eye fucking him.

"What you do to my niece, man?"

"Nigga, what yo' loud ass do? You woke her up with all that yelling!" Yara huffed as she finished changing Coco's diaper and lifted her in her arms, only for Psalm to come swoop her away.

"My bad, Uncle Psalm ain't mean to wake his fat mama up." He used a baby voice and peppered her chubby cheek with loud kisses.

"Ugh! Don't put yo' lips on my baby face! I don't know where them muthafuckas been!"

"Man, quit playin' with me. Niecy poo the only person on this planet getting access to these lips," his mean ass grumbled, mugging her. Yara smacked her lips and waved him off.

"Anyway, you remember Amari, don't you?" She grinned mischievously, drawing his eyes my way, and I made up in my mind that I was going to pinch her ass as soon as I got the chance to. I wiggled my fingers at him dryly, getting annoyed by his silence as he just stared at me.

"Mmhm," he only grunted, and I was grateful when the boys ran in disrupting the awkward moment.

"What's up, Unc!" SJ immediately jumped on Psalm and the mug I thought was permanently attached to his face split into a wide grin as he dapped him up.

"What's up lil' homie? Who's yo' friend?" he asked, noticing Prince who was standing by the door quietly.

"He Prince!" SJ happily announced.

"Young Prince, I like that." Psalm nodded, lifting his fist, and Prince damn near tripped over himself to hit it. I watched as they had a conversation and was surprised at how easily my baby had taken to him. Prince didn't usually talk to strangers like that, but I was guessing he was more comfortable with Psalm because he was SJ's uncle. I finished packing and had our ride home scheduled while they talked. When it said our car was only a few minutes away, I tucked my phone in my pocket and lifted my bag.

"Come on Prince, our ride will be here soon, baby." The way his face fell as he came over and grabbed the hand I held out for him broke my heart. My baby didn't get to play with other kids outside of daycare like that, so he was really excited to hang out with SJ and it was obvious. Hopefully he'd get the chance to again real soon.

"Girl, I am not letting you ride no Uber home. Just give me a second and—" Yara started, but I was already shaking my head.

"I can't ask you to drag the baby out right now. Besides, my ride already on the way."

She narrowed her eyes as I spoke, already getting her argument ready. "Psalm can take you then, he ain't doin' shit." She shrugged and we both shot her a look.

"Man, how you know what I got goin' on?" he quickly argued with his nose turned up.

"It's okay, really—"

"See, she said it's cool." Psalm's relief was all over his face, irritating me for some reason. It was like he couldn't stand me even though I'd only been around his black ass all of two times. I resisted the urge to roll my eyes and instead pulled out my phone like I'd gotten a notification.

"Yeah, my ride already pulling up anyway," I lied, ignoring the side eye Yara was giving me. "Thanks for today tho'."

"Girl please, thank you. I love it! Shit, speaking of which, let me pay you before I forget." She rushed over to her phone, and a second later, my Cash app was alerting me of a payment. I thanked her again but didn't even stop to see how much she'd sent before rushing to leave just as Saint came in the door. He seemed surprised to see me, but Yara came out into the hallway, drawing his attention.

"Where the fuck have you been?" she immediately went off, and I used the opportunity to slip past him and outside to safety. I already knew it was about to be some shit because I'd had that same conversation with Malik more times than I could count, and I was glad I was done with that shit. Unfortunately, I was left just standing outside though, because my ride was still in route.

"Mommy, it's hot," Prince complained as we sat down on the steps to wait. Before I could reply, though, Psalm stepped out with his face still balled up. I really couldn't understand how somebody could walk around with an attitude all the time. Yara had said he'd gone through some shit that made him such an asshole, but it had to be something serious for how extra he was with it. As soon as I realized it was him, I rolled my eyes, too hot to bother with pretending.

"I thought yo' ride was here?" He surprised me by speaking. I started not to say shit back and treat him like he'd been treating me, but instead, I shrugged.

"I guess I read the message wrong." I kept my eyes straight forward, hoping he'd take his ass on, but when he eventually scoffed and started down the steps, I glared at his back. I could already imagine that the Range Rover he was walking to had a good AC, and as if reading my thoughts, my baby nudged me.

"I'm hoooooot!" I quickly tried to shush him, but it was too late. Psalm had already heard his little loud ass. He stopped on the passenger side and pulled the door open.

"Come on, I'll take you," he said in that gruff tone I was beginning to hate so much, and I shook my head.

"We're fine, the car gone be here soon—"

"Man, get yo' difficult ass in the car before shorty have a heat stroke," he snapped, walking around to the driver's side and leaving the passenger door open like he just knew I was coming. I was going to let his goofy ass just sit there with the door open like a fool, but one look at my baby's sweaty face had me sighing before walking him over to the truck and praying that I didn't have to curse him out.

Yara

"What the fuck was she doin' here?" Saint had the nerve to question me as soon as the door closed behind Psalm. He may have really wanted to know why Amari was there, but I had a feeling he was trying to avoid telling me where he'd been. Saint was good at distracting me to get himself out of shit, but I wasn't falling for it this time.

"No, the question is, why are *you* just now getting here? Last I heard, you were at an open mic night. That shit take that long?" I asked, cocking my head up at him. Despite being pissed off and wanting to slap the taste out his mouth, I couldn't help marveling at how fucking gorgeous he was. God had really done his big one when he made my man, but it was becoming a curse though because he was famous and fine, or rather rich and fine.

Being the face of Savage Records, he always wanted to be out and about splurging and showing off. At first I was right by his side, tossing money in the clubs and shopping every day, but with SJ I slowed down a lot, and now with Coco I was at a full stop. I still did my shit occasionally but nowhere near as much as Saint, and damn sure not enough to keep me out all night. I didn't want to think the worst because most often than not, he was working, looking for new talent, or out showcasing the talent on his roster, but there were times I wasn't so sure that was all he was doing.

Despite the rumors, I'd never caught Saint cheating on me and while I was grateful for that, I was still suspicious when he pulled shit like this. I eyed him from head to toe, looking for some type of sign that he was up to no good but came up short as always. Either he really wasn't doing anything or he was good at what he did do.

"Damn Yara, after the show I ended up going to the club with Flex and them niggas." I squinted as he explained, not sure whether I should believe him or not.

"So, you want me to believe you been in the club all night?"

"Naw man, I fell asleep at Flex crib." He seemed unfazed by my tone as he swaggered over to where I stood, still holding Coco. Dropping a kiss on her head, he wrapped his arms around me but I ducked his puckered lips. "Damn, you still trippin'? What you want me to call that nigga or something?" He leaned back with an attitude, eyebrows bunched.

"For what, so he can lie for you? I don't believe shit that nigga say!"

"You tweakin' bro. If you don't think I was where I said I was, then call him! What the fuck that nigga gotta lie for me for?" he huffed, and I looked at his ass like he was crazy. There were plenty of reasons that Flex's weed-head ass would lie for him, the most important one being that Saint was his boss. He was a yes man and basically did whatever Saint and Psalm told him to, and if they asked him for an alibi for the murder, he'd be the first one up at the police station, so lying about where Saint was last night wasn't shit. Instead of stating the obvious, I just sucked my teeth and wiggled out of his grip as SJ came running out.

"Hey Daddy!" He pushed himself between me and his father, unaware of the tense moment he'd just interrupted.

"What's up mini me!" Saint picked him up with ease, tickling his belly. As bad as I couldn't stand his lying ass at the moment, I smiled seeing him with SJ. He was a great father to our children no matter how fucked up of a fiancé he was to me. Even Coco was cracking up and clapping at them playing in front of us. When Saint noticed, he set SJ down and took her out of my arms, blowing raspberries into her neck. It was a scene straight out of a Hallmark movie, but I felt like a viewer instead of the leading female character.

While they continued playing, I slipped up the stairs so I could take a shower and cool off. With the way Saint was so wrapped up in his record label and hanging out, it was few and far between that I got a moment to myself these days. I enjoyed being a full-time mom, but I was beginning to think it was time to get a nanny since Saint's ass hadn't been much help. Our parents did as much as they could, watching them while both of us worked unless I was doing videos or something from home. The few hours that SJ spent at school helped, but most of my club appearances or modeling gigs were on the weekend when he was home, so that really didn't do much. If anything, having a nanny to tag along when I was out with the kids would take some of the load off, and I made a mental note to look into it once I finished my shower.

Knowing that my time was limited before one or both of the kids would be hungry or something, I started the water and stripped out of my clothes. My hair was already pulled up, but I still added a shower cap since I still needed to make an actual video about the wig I was wearing and I wanted it to look as fresh as possible.

I stepped under the hot water and turned around so it was hitting my back and shoulders with just the right amount of pressure. The tension I'd been feeling started to fade a little, but a second later it returned when the door came open. Saint stood there looking at me through the glass, and I rolled my eyes as he started removing his clothes.

"Where are the kids?" I huffed, ready to get right back out once he climbed in with me. The little moment I was trying to steal was already ruined the minute he invaded the bathroom anyway, so it wouldn't have been a big deal to shower later.

"My OG down there, she bouta take them for the night." He stopped me, looping his arm around my waist.

"Well I need to go get their stuff ready—"

"Damn Ya, she got it. You actin' like she don't know what she doin' or somethin'. Finish yo' shower, man." Sighing, I backed out of his reach and snatched up my pink loofah with an attitude. It wasn't like he was wrong, Angel knew everything about our kids and even had some things for them at her house. I really just wanted to get the fuck away from Saint.

With my back to him, I lathered my body, ignoring him sucking his teeth and grumbling behind me as he did the same, but I wasn't about to feed into his shit. He still hadn't made any attempt to explain his whereabouts, so he had to know I was still irritated with his presence. The smell of his soap overpowering my own even irritated me and I rushed to finish. After washing and rinsing off for the third time, I hung my loofah back up and moved to get out, but Saint came up behind me.

Trapping me between him and the shower door, he pressed his dick in my back and softly bit my shoulder. "You really bouta get out without lettin' me feel that pussy, Ya?" His hand slipped between my thighs, stopping once he reached my clit. It had been a couple of days since I'd gotten my pussy stroked, so it definitely felt good, but the fact that I wasn't sure what he was doing the night before was nagging at me.

"You really not gone tell me where you were last night?" I shot back, making him groan lowly.

"*Baby*...you feel how hard my dick is right now and you wanna argue. I already told you I was with Flex." As he spoke, he put pressure on my clit, and I squeezed my thighs together, unable to stop my body from responding. "You think I'd be fucked up enough to come in here, tryna fuck you after I been cheating all night?"

The logic behind that question was stupid. A nigga would do anything to cover his tracks, and I didn't think Saint was any different, but I must have been thinking with my pussy at the moment because, for some reason, that shit made sense. He sucked my earlobe into his mouth and my stomach clenched from the double stimulation. Saint knew that was my spot and I grinded against his hand, quickly coating his fingers with my juices. His dick twitched, growing harder as he let out a low moan.

"Damn Ya, you want daddy in that pussy bad, huh?" He removed his hand from between my legs and instantly brought his fingers to his mouth.

"*Yes*!" I whimpered, still feeling the effects of my orgasm.

"Touch them fuckin' toes then." His voice was gruff as he backed away, giving me just enough room to do what he'd told me. Without hesitation, I wrapped one hand around my ankle and pressed the other one against the wall. My pussy throbbed with anticipation, and I tucked my lip between my teeth, trying to bite back a moan. I quickly lost that battle when I felt Saint's tongue snake between my folds.

"Mmmm, *baby*." My knees buckled as he gripped my thighs and hungrily attacked my clit. I could see him stroking his length and I shuddered, getting more turned on by the pre cum oozing from the tip. The sound of him slurping up my juices and his groans of pleasure echoed off the shower walls.

"That's right, grind this juicy muthafucka on my tongue, Ya," he ordered, sucking my clit in his mouth between each word. My heart pounded and I felt a tingling sensation rising through my body, an indication that another orgasm was near.

"*Fuck, fuck, fuck*! I'mboutacum babe!" My words came out jumbled as Saint got extra sloppy with it. I tried to lock my knees in an attempt to stop myself from falling over but it did little to help.

"Don't tap out on me now, wifey." Saint smacked my ass cheek as he stood to his full height. "I'm bouta punish this lil' pussy." That was the only warning I got before he buried himself deep in my walls. He cursed under his breath and gripped the back of my neck, giving it a light squeeze as he pulled out only to slam back into me.

"Ooh, *Saint*! You soo fuckin' deep!" I finally found my words, enjoying every delicious inch he was delivering to me. He slapped my ass again, picking up speed as I clenched my muscles around him.

"This dick belong to you, Ya. Stamp yo' name on this muhfucka," he ordered, hitting my spot relentlessly. His dick grew harder, expanding as I threw my ass back on him, and I knew he was on the verge of nutting. Both of his hands found my waist and his movements became stiff. I was right there with him and my toes curled as he massaged my asshole, sending me over the edge. I shook uncontrollably and my eyes rolled back into my head when I finally climaxed. If Saint wasn't holding on to me I probably would've crumpled to the floor. That's just how strong it was, and not even a second later he was filling me up. With his dick still pumping inside me, Saint sat back on the shower bench, pulling me along with him, which I was grateful for because my legs felt like they were asleep. We sat there for a few minutes as we recovered with Saint pressing soft kisses on my neck and shoulders.

The shower water was just barely lukewarm when we were finally able to move again, and we washed up quickly before retreating to our bedroom. After moisturizing my body, I selected a shirt from his closet and as soon as he saw me, he laughed. "I know damn well you got some expensive ass pajamas in those drawers, bro."

"So, I like your shirts better." I shrugged, getting comfortable under the covers because I was suddenly tired as hell. With my hand propped under my chin, I watched him shake his head as he slipped on a wife beater and some boxer briefs. My eyes settled on the bulge below his waist even though he had just put my pussy through a beating.

"You might as well stop looking at my shit, it got the rest of the night off." He climbed in bed with me, with his phone in hand. "We bouta enjoy this kid-free night, order some food, and rent a movie or some shit, and you gone take yo' horny ass to sleep."

He was already looking up food places as butterflies swam in my belly, and I couldn't stop a smile from emerging. This was the Saint I had missed so much. The one that would rather chill at home with me than go out to different clubs. It had been a while since he'd wanted to just spend time with me, without the kids, and I couldn't lie. I was excited.

"I'm good with that," I noted, and he shot me a playful mug.

"You better be, the fuck!" Reaching over, he tickled me to the point that I cracked up laughing.

"Okay, okay, I'm good with dinner and a movie, but you better make it worth it too."

"Any time with me is worth it, girl. You better act like you know." Rolling my eyes at him poking his chest out, I snuggled up against him. Pleased for the night in, I let my earlier worry go and focused on laying up with my man.

Saint

I ignored another call from Koi and made sure my shit was set to silent. I was in a whole ass meeting, and her goofy ass was blowing me up like it was an emergency when she was just pissed about being ignored. After seeing the way my bullshit was affecting Yara, I was trying to put some distance between me and Koi, but she was making that shit hard. It had barely been twenty-four hours and she was sending me pictures of her playing in her pussy and saying she missed me. I guess it made sense that she'd be worried so quickly. In the few months we'd been fucking around, I hadn't gone a day without seeing or talking to her, so me ghosting her ass was probably throwing her for a loop.

I could feel Psalm's eyes on me, but I ignored him too. If he knew that Koi was turning into a stalker overnight, he'd have a whole lot to say and I wasn't trying to hear that shit. He already had too much of an opinion and it was annoying as hell, and if he found out he was right his little lectures would only get worse.

"So, y'all wanna sign me? What y'all contracts look like? How much of an advance would I get if I fuck with y'all? 'Cause I heard that nigga Flex got almost a hundred bands." This nigga Malice tossed out question after question, and I shot a look at my brother. I could already read the look on his face and he wasn't feeling that nigga. Psalm had been impressed by his performance, but his mug had been present since Malice sat down and opened his mouth. In just the last thirty minutes he'd bragged about how many hoes he had, inquired about whether or not child support could be taken out of an advance, and wanted to order the most expensive bottle the club had to offer. He even had me looking at his ass sideways from some of the shit he'd let come out his mouth, and I was the laid-back brother. His manager had tried to get him to tone it down but he either had to be drunk or off a pill, 'cause he was doing too much.

The way Psalm sat up and scratched his head, I already knew he was about to insult that nigga so I tried to speak before he could. "Actually—"

"Actually," Psalm cut me off, resting his elbows on his knees. "We just came to see you perform live. I don't know what the fuck this nigga told you." He snorted and nodded toward Malice's manager, Kenneth. "Now do I think you got potential? Maybe. You only got one song that muhfuckas actually listen to, and that's the one Dola helped you with, right?"

"Yeah, but—"

"That means yo' pen game need a whole lot of work. Shit, you probably gone need a ghost writer to actually get a hit if we keeping it real. When you get that handled, then maybe you should hit us up, but until then, I'ma have to respectfully decline."

Fuck! This nigga did more than just insult my guy, his ass went for the jugular and basically said he was talentless. I braced myself, waiting for Malice to get on some tough guy shit so we could beat him and his manager's asses, but they both just sat there in disbelief. They probably hadn't seen shit going that way when they sat down. I damn sure hadn't.

An uncomfortable silence fell over the table, and Malice looked my way in uncertainty but I didn't know what to tell his ass. Psalm didn't even give that nigga a chance to recover though, lifting his drink as he sat back smoothly.

"Y'all can go now," he dismissed, and I quickly tried to lessen the blow.

"We'll be in touch if anything changes." I stood and extended my hand even as Psalm burned a hole in the side of my face. It took a second, but Kenneth finally got the hint and climbed to his feet, prompting Malice to as well.

"Man, fuck y'all! They ain't stop making record labels when y'all made Savage! Y'all shit ain't even got good artists! Fuck outta here!" Malice spat, slapping my hand away. His bitch ass tried to walk off, but I caught him by his shirt and yoked him up.

"Boy, I'll—"

"Man, let his lil' bitch ass go, this nigga a walkin' lawsuit!" Psalm appeared at my side and my jaw clenched as I contemplated his words. I knew my brother was right and the second he got a chance, he'd run his ass to the nearest lawyer and try to have me in court. Sneering, I released him with a shove and he fell into Kenneth. I stood there mugging them as Kenneth dragged him away, talking shit like I was supposed to be scared. "Sit yo' big ass down fool, that nigga ain't comin' back and you ain't bouta have Yara in my face 'cause you fucked around and got locked up."

Begrudgingly, I dropped back down on the couch next to him, with my face still balled up. "That nigga smacked my fuckin' hand like I was a lil' ass kid!" I was still pissed off but for some reason, Psalm thought the shit was funny.

"He did smack the fuck out yo' shit tho'!" he chuckled, sparking up a blunt.

"Yeah, he should've did that shit to yo' ass, you're the one that was comin' at him crazy."

"He was the one talkin' crazy. Askin' 'bout advances and child support and shit. Where the fuck you find his goofy ass anyway?" I took the blunt he extended to me and snorted.

"He was on some mixtape with Dola that Koi's ass was listening to." That information had Psalm's face screwed up like it did whenever Koi's name came out my mouth.

"This bitch," he grumbled lowly as my phone lit up on the

table. I already knew without looking that it was Koi again, and I dreaded whatever the fuck she'd sent this time. "That's who calls you duckin'?" His intuitive ass knew the answer without me even having to say, and I snatched up my phone to see that it was in fact Koi with another message. It was a long ass paragraph that I wasn't about to read. Instead, I checked to see if Yara had tried to reach me, and when I saw that she hadn't, I shoved my phone down in my pocket.

"Yo' ass gone get enough," he warned.

"You ain't gotta keep sayin' that shit bro, I get it. The other day Yara was on one 'cause my dumb ass stayed out all night." His eyes bucked and he choked on the weed.

"Nigga—"

"I already know, I just got caught up on some drunk shit. I ain't fuckin' with her ass no more tho', that's why she blowin' me up like this." Psalm was already shaking his head.

"You better hope she ain't on no fatal attraction shit," he warned. "Fuck around and lose yo' wife and yo' side bitch."

"Nigga, is you tryna convince me to leave her alone or not, ole' confusin' ass." I side eyed him, snatching the weed before he could hit it again. Every time I talked to him, he was trying to tell me to stop fucking with her, and now that I had, he was warning me about her ass being crazy. Koi could act stupid if she wanted to, but I wasn't like niggas in the movies. I'd fuck around and kill her ass the first time she did some nutty shit.

Psalm held his hands up in mock surrender. "You know I'm team Yara all day, I just don't want her to be blindsided by a rabbit boilin', bacon burnin' side bitch."

"Nigga *what*!"

He looked at me like I had a comprehension problem before shaking his head. "Never mind, bro. I'm just sayin', I don't want sis to end up having to slide a hoe 'cause you don't know how to keep yo' dick to yo' self."

"If she knows what's good for her, she'll stay her monkey ass out Yara's face! My girl ain't gone be out here fightin' nobody 'cause I'll catch a case behind the future Mrs. Savage." I honestly hadn't considered Koi approaching my girl on some goofy shit, mostly because she didn't seem like the type. She was all about her money, so I was hoping she'd just move on to the next nigga lining her pockets and leave me alone. Hell, if I was lucky, her baby daddy would spin the block and take her mind off me, but if by chance that didn't happen, I'd have to handle shit another way.

"Now yo' ass out here threatening hoes and shit! Wait till I tell Mama, ole dirty dick nigga."

"Man, fuck you!" I grumbled. His ass stayed throwing shots and trying to threaten me with telling our OG whenever I did something. My mama didn't play about certain shit and hitting women was at the very top of her list. One time I'd hemmed Yara up while we were at her house and she came out hitting me with a damn spatula like I was a little boy. She chased me around her crib for a half hour and only stopped because she had to check on the food she was cooking. He was there that day so he knew she'd act a fool if he told her that shit. I stood up, ready to go, and that only seemed to amuse his goofy ass more.

"Where you goin'? Bet not be to that hoe house, or I'll have something else to tell Mama!" he cracked, looking up at me with a grin as smoke seeped from his nose.

"I'm goin' home to my girl, some shit yo' miserable ass don't know shit about. You'd probably be in a better mood if you got some pussy yo' damn self." I left his ass sitting and headed out to my car.

I was suddenly missing my woman, and that was crazy because I hadn't felt like that in a long time, but instead of sitting there with him any longer, I was going to lay up. As I headed out to my car, I nodded to a few people who shouted out my name, and I was glad not to see any muthafuckas with cameras when I made it outside. It was probably due to the spot being low key, but with the way people liked to record on their phones, it wouldn't be long before somebody's reporting agency pulled up.

"Saint! Saint, baby wait!"

I cringed as soon as I heard Koi's ass behind me. I started to ignore her, but I didn't want her to keep yelling my name and calling me baby and risk somebody else hearing her. The sound of her heels clacking against the pavement let me know how close she'd gotten to me, and by the time I turned around, she was only a few feet away. "What the fuck you out here screaming for!"

"Baby—" I snatched her ass by the arm as soon as she was within reach and dragged her out of the view of anybody else.

"What you doin' here, Koi? You following me or some shit?" Her eyes were already wide from the way I'd grabbed her, but they damn near popped out of her head at that.

"One of my followers said you were here for open mic, so I showed up since you won't answer my calls!" She got louder, damn near whining. "What's wrong with you? Why you been ghosting me all day?" She rubbed my chest affectionately, looking up at me with puppy dog eyes.

I hadn't intended to say anything to her about breaking things off. I was honestly just going to let her figure that shit out on her own, but I also wasn't planning on seeing her ass again so soon. Now I was trapped with her crazy ass in a dark parking lot and didn't have a choice.

"Look, we need to chill out for a minute." I tried to keep the agitation out of my voice as I spoke, lifting her hand. She watched in confusion as I removed it from my chest like that shit was contaminated.

"Wh-what? Why?" She became frantic despite the kid gloves I was trying to use. "Did I do something?"

I sighed, seeing that this shit wasn't going as smoothly as I thought it would. "No, you ain't do shit. I'm just tryna get shit right with my fiancée." In the few seconds we'd been standing there, I'd thought of a couple of reasons to give her but ultimately went with the truth, hoping it'd produce better results, but judging from the mug on her face, it didn't work. Cocking her head, Koi looked up at me with narrowed eyes.

"You're breaking up with me for yo' baby mama!" She frowned, jerking her head back.

"I'm just fuckin' you girl, ain't no breaking up! We were just fuckin' and now I don't wanna fuck you no more 'cause I'm bouta get married! Fuck is wrong with you!"

"So you take every girl you just fuckin' all over the city of Chicago? And on business trips when your precious *baby mama* is too busy? You tryna make it seem like you don't fuck with me like that but you definitely fuck with me more than her!" I grabbed her arms and shook her stupid ass.

"*Shut up*!" I shouted, catching myself as a group of people walked past the parking lot laughing loudly.

"Fuck you, Saint!" Koi scratched at my hands and I let her go before she had me looking like I'd been picking up stray cats. Her eyes were wild as she backed away from me, and as soon as she had enough distance, she raised both her middle fingers before scurrying back toward the street. After she was out of sight, I considered how much better it had gone than I thought it would. I'd lowkey been expecting for her to show her ass, try to blast me, or some other crazy ass shit. It wasn't the cleanest break, but it was done, and I wouldn't have to worry about her.

Amari

I watched my baby daddy's latest video and rolled my eyes. For the last week, he'd been going live after dropping a diss track about Savage Records and their artists. Apparently, he'd gotten disrespected by them and wanted to expose them to the world. I saw right through this shit though, already knowing it was a gimmick for views. It was definitely the most attention he'd received in a while, but it put me in a fucked-up position because of my blossoming friendship with Yara. I just hoped they didn't think I had shit to do with my baby daddy's antics.

"Ugh, that boy still going?" My mama peeked over my shoulder at the phone screen and shook her head. "That shit don't make no sense. The way these rappers getting killed out here, he knows he needs to stop."

Shrugging, I exited out of Instagram and set my phone aside. "I would try to talk to him but Prince never gave him a reason to act right, so I doubt if anything I say will stop him." I still hadn't even talked to Malik since he'd ghosted me on the daycare payment. I'd been too busy to even think about him since the video I'd done with Yara. Already, I had so many new hair and makeup clients that I was having to turn some of them away. There was a bigger demand for videos on my channel and the views were going up on all my old ones. I'd gained thousands of new followers and I'd gotten my first paid advertisement, so Malik had been the last thing on my mind.

Now since his ass was all over the internet talking shit about Saint and Psalm, there was a big chance that it could backfire on me. Considering how much I'd gained in the short amount of time since I'd linked up with Yara, there was no way I was ready to lose it behind my baby daddy.

"Well, somebody better tell him something, 'cause if my grandbaby get caught up in his shit, I'm gone kill his ass myself!" my mama vowed, and I didn't put it past her. Myra Sinclair might have been a small woman, but she was just as crazy as any of these street niggas when it came to her family.

"I don't think the people he's talking about are like that, Ma." My defense was weak because I didn't know shit about what Saint or Psalm would do, especially since I'd only been around them a couple of times. They were assholes for sure, but were they the type that would shoot a nigga down for running his mouth? That I didn't know. Even when Psalm had given me a ride home that day he'd made no attempt at conversation. The whole ride was just silent besides the music he had playing, with his rude ass. His little one-sided beef with me was already annoying. I didn't want to give him another reason to hate me by way of my baby daddy, though.

"Baby, it ain't just the rappers out here killin' each other, it's regular ass niggas tryna make a name for themselves."

"Well, since one of the dudes he's talkin' about is Yara's fiancée, I'll see if I can smooth things over on my end, but I don't think it'll be a be deal. It ain't like Malik ever picks Prince up anyway." My mama's nose wrinkled as she thought about the truth of my statement before nodding.

"True. You definitely got you an ain't shit baby daddy! That's for sure!"

"Dang, Ma," I gasped in mock offense. "Tell me how you really feel."

"Shit, it's true." She walked off, slippers sliding across the wood floor and making that obnoxious ass noise. I decided to let her make it though. She was in the middle of cooking some fried chicken, cheese rice, and string beans, and my mouth was watering just waiting for it. My phone buzzing against the table had my heart racing when I saw Yara's name flashing on my screen. I looked behind me for my mama like some type of backup, but she'd already disappeared into the kitchen. Taking a deep breath, I slid the icon across the screen and braced myself for whatever she was about to say.

"Hey, girl!" I tried not to sound as anxious as I really was.

"Hey, boo, I called you for a couple things." Her voice was very business oriented, but I noticed that it wasn't angry, which slightly put me at ease. "First, SJ wanted to know when Prince can come back over 'cause he's lonely." She dropped the professional tone she was using and we both snickered at SJ's dramatics.

"Well, we can't have that," I teased. "Prince has been asking about him too, girl. I think we done started something."

"We definitely did, but if y'all free tomorrow I can come get you and we can take them somewhere to burn off some of that boy energy."

"Ummm, let me make sure." I stalled as I put her on speaker so that I could check my calendar. The fact that I even had to do something like that felt amazing, and I was glad to see that I didn't have anything booked for the next day, which I told her and we settled on being ready by noon.

"Okay, so for the other reason I called." She dragged the word thoughtfully, and I wondered what she was about to say. "I have an event coming up and I was just wondering if you wanted to come with me?" My eyes widened because that was the last thing I was expecting. Despite what she'd said about coming back over or whatever, I still thought that was just something people said with no real intentions of following through. It was cool that she wasn't that type of IT girl though. "It's just one of those day parties where they take pictures and network, so nothing too major."

"Oh hell yeah!" I said excitedly, already thinking of what I would wear and what I would move around just so that I could go.

"Great! We can go over the details tomorrow and I'll see you at 12."

"See you then girl, bye."

"Bye."

As soon as the call disconnected, I let out an excited squeal that had my mama running in from the kitchen. "What! What is it!" She held a spatula like she was about squash a bug or something.

"You know that girl whose hair I just did not too long ago? Well, she just called and invited me to a day party with her!" I made the same noise as she waved me off with a mug.

"Girl! I thought something was wrong! Don't be making all that damn noise in here. What the hell wrong with you!"

"My bad, Ma." I toned down but still couldn't stop the biggest smile from spreading across my face. I was really moving up in the world and I couldn't wait!

The next day came quickly, and as stated, me and Prince were ready by eleven thirty. He was in his room playing while I sat on the couch looking over the numbers on my latest post. It seemed like every day my following was growing, and I was more than a little appreciative of Yara. In just a couple of weeks she'd looked out for me more than people I'd known longer, and I made a mental note to grab her something cute as a way to say thank you.

A knock at the door brought me out of my thoughts, and I frowned seeing that I hadn't gotten a text from Yara. I hadn't planned on her coming upstairs when she arrived. Although my apartment was clean and cute for a girl with a budget, it was a far cry from the one she lived in with Saint. Then again, everybody knew Yara came from humble beginnings, and the type of person she was, I doubted if she treated me any differently. With that thought in mind, I went to answer it and was surprised to see Koi on the other side. We hadn't talked since the day I did Yara's hair so I figured she had an attitude with me. I tried to keep my face neutral even though I was feeling a way about that phony shit.

"Hey girl, what you doin' here?" I asked cautiously, taking in her appearance. She was dressed down in leggings and a t-shirt with her hair tucked under a Nike hat. Obviously, something was wrong for her to be dressed so plain. I still hadn't stepped aside so she could come in, and instead of waiting for me to do so, she just brushed past me.

"Damn, since when do I need to have a reason to see my bestie?" She dropped her purse on the coffee table and sat down, raising her brow at me. I could instantly tell something was off about her demeanor, but I couldn't really put my finger on it, and at the moment, I really didn't have much time to.

"I was just wondering since you didn't call or anything." Letting the door close, I followed her over to the couch and sat in the same spot I'd been in before she got there. She hummed her answer, looking around the room like she'd never been there before. "Me and Prince were about to head out soon." Her nose turned up and she finally looked at me, noticing for the first time that I was dressed.

"Where the hell y'all going? If anything, y'all need to be staying in since yo' dumb ass baby daddy decided to wage war on Savage Records," she said dryly, and I rolled my eyes. Of course, she'd know about the shit that Malik was out here doing, but had yet to like a single one of my latest videos. Still, I hesitated to tell her that I was going on a play date with Yara. She'd already had a fit when I linked up with her for business, so I already knew this was going to be an issue.

"Me and Yara are taking the boys out for the day." I tried to shrug like it was no big deal, but she jerked back like I'd slapped her.

"*Yara?*" she said her name like it tasted bitter on her tongue. "Y'all friends or something now? I thought you were just doing her hair for promotion, not kickin' it with her and her son." She seemed particularly annoyed, looking at me like I was a traitor or something.

"I wouldn't say friends, but we're cool." Yara hadn't put a label on our linking up, but I wasn't going to act like I didn't fuck with her. How could I not? In just a couple of weeks she'd hooked me up, and I had to admit I actually liked her a lot. Koi's nose turned up like she smelled shit, and I rolled my eyes at her dramatics.

"And now y'all planning play dates and shit? That's weird, Amari, especially when you know I'm messing with her baby daddy!"

"I don't have shit to do with you and Saint's mess. Our kids like hanging out and Yara cool as hell, ain't nothin' *weird* about it," I told her, but she was already shaking her head.

"You really gonna try and make it seem cool that you and that bitch hanging out? She's cool now, but what you think she gone do when she finds out you're friends with the bitch that's been fuckin' her nigga?" She gave me a pointed look before laughing bitterly. "Between that and the shit Malik been doin', you're really her biggest opp besides me, but if you wanna pretend y'all besties, then I guess."

I couldn't lie. What she was saying bothered me, mostly because there was some truth to it despite the bitterness behind her words. Those were things I was already considering, but at the same time, I'd only just found out about Saint and Koi. It wasn't like I was out doing double dates with them or booking them hotels to fuck around in. And as far as Malik, I didn't have shit to do with what his crazy ass had going on. Me and my son reaped no benefits from him any day of the year, and we damn sure weren't going to see a dime from his latest publicity stunt. I guessed what really nagged at me was how she seemed like she'd be happy if Yara found out and stopped fucking with me. I mean, damn, I knew she didn't like the girl, but I was her best friend and she was talking to me like I'd intentionally gone out and befriended Yara. If anything, Koi was the one who brought us together with her sneaky ass games, so it was really her fault. Instead of calling her out, though, I decided to find out what was really her issue because something was making her act so nasty, and it wasn't just my relationship with Yara.

"Girl, what did you come over here for? 'Cause I know it wasn't to talk shit about me and Yara." My tone wiped the smug look off her face and she rolled her eyes.

"It was to talk to my best friend, but I guess I don't have one of those here." She jumped to her feet to make her dramatic exit, and I twisted my lips, taking my time to stand as well. I really couldn't deal with Koi when she got in her moods like this, so the best thing for her to do was leave and fast before we started really going in on each other. I didn't know about her, but I still considered her a friend and I didn't want either of us to say some shit we couldn't take back.

She beat me to the door and let herself out and a second later, Yara was texting to let me know she was a few minutes away. "Prince, come on, baby, it's time to go!" I called, and Prince came running out of his room thirstily. The smile on his face knowing that he was about to see SJ put the bullshit Koi was talking about to the back of my mind. We were going to enjoy the day, fuck what she was talking about.

Psalm

"You hear this shit, man? You gotta let me put out a response." Flex and another one of our artists named Vito were currently in my office trying to convince me to let them do a diss for Malice. I'd been against engaging with that lame ass nigga off the strength that he was clearly a bitch, but they felt otherwise.

"Yeah bro, we over here lookin' like Drake after the Kendrick diss, and don't nobody wanna be that nigga right now," Vito added, shaking his head, and I bit back a laugh. He was definitely right, but at the same time, I didn't want this shit to escalate because I'd fuck around and have to kill that little nigga. It had been years since I'd done any type of street shit that could put me behind bars, but the ability never went away. Malice had the ability to bring out the beast that I'd kept at bay, and I didn't want that. Shit, nobody wanted that if I was being honest.

"Look, that nigga just tryna get his lil' fifteen minutes of fame right now. He's getting a little traction, but it's nowhere near the level y'all on. Y'all really tryna step off yo' throne to spar with that non-rapping ass nigga?"

"Hell yeah!"

"Hell yeah!"

They said at the same time, and I couldn't do shit but shake my head. "Ayite man, I'll get y'all a beat and y'all better come with bars or I'ma fire y'all niggas," I teased, making them immediately start talking shit. I already knew they were going to demolish that nigga, but it didn't hurt to light a fire under their asses either.

"You got us fucked up!"

I shrugged, tossing my hands up. "I'm just sayin', his non' rappin' ass kinda fucked you up with that bar about yo' baby mama," I told Vito, and his face balled up as he grumbled under his breath, waving me and Flex off.

"On some real shit, that nigga got a baby mama too and his ass don't even claim her. He keeps her ass in hiding, but I remember her being around when he first started out. She bad too, but I'll still roast the fuck out her fine ass! I don't give a fuck!" Vito said, and I suddenly remembered him asking us about child support. That nigga never mentioned any kids or a baby mama in his raps or the few interviews he'd done, and that made me look at him even worse now, 'cause what type of nigga didn't claim his baby? I didn't know how he'd gotten her to keep quiet about being his baby mama either, because most rapper's BMs loved to be seen, but then again, she was probably embarrassed by that nigga. He had been rapping for years and even after his right hand had been put on, he still wasn't getting anywhere. That shit had to be embarrassing and if I was him, I would've quit a long ass time ago.

"No he don't," Flex argued in disbelief. Shit, I wouldn't have believed it either if I hadn't heard him talking about child support.

"Nigga," Vito started, pulling his phone out while I looked on with a raised brow. Whatever he was looking for didn't take long to find, and seconds later, he was tossing it over to Flex. "Told yo' ass! That's his baby mama!" He sat back proudly and Flex covered his mouth in shock, eyes wide as he analyzed whatever he was looking at. Now I was really interested. Whoever shorty was had

Flex's loud mouth ass stunned silent, and that was a hard feat because he never shut up.

He sat up to hand the phone over to me with a nod. "She's definitely fine as hell. What the fuck she was doin' lettin' that broke ass nigga hit?" he questioned Vito while I finally laid my eyes on the picture and was hit with the beautiful face of Amari. It was obviously from a few years ago but it was definitely her, and she was smiling hard while Malice's bitch ass hugged her from behind, holding the small pudge in her belly. Next to them stood Dola and that bitch Koi, and they were all standing underneath a marquee with his and Malice's names. I hadn't seen that shit coming. I didn't know how Flex hadn't recognized her, but he was fucked up the night we met. Of all the women in Chicago to be tied to that nigga, I hadn't expected it to be Amari, but the wheels in my head were already spinning. Malice might've been trying to hide her ass, but he it wasn't because he didn't think that was his baby, or he wouldn't have been worried about her putting him on child support. Regardless of the act he was putting on, I was sure he gave a fuck about his baby mama. That picture solidified it. What was worse than a nigga talking shit about you? A nigga fucking your baby mama while he did it. Malice didn't know it yet, but I was about to have him ready for a straitjacket.

I handed Vito his phone back as I considered how I was about to do this shit. With her hanging around Yara, she'd be accessible. I just needed to not make it so obvious what I was doing. "Hold off on putting her in the diss, I got something better in mind," I said, and Flex's eyes widened.

"You not bouta fuck that nigga BM, is you? That's some disrespectful ass shit right there!"

"Nah, I'ma just keep her in my back pocket. Just don't tell nobody about this shit. Work on the track and I'll handle her," I told him, hoping his goofy ass didn't get fucked up and let this shit slip to anybody. They both nodded and I shooed them off so I could iron out the details.

I'd had a few days to consider the angle I was going to approach Amari with, but I was still coming up short. We had only been around each other a handful of times, and I hadn't shown any interest in talking to her, so I couldn't get at her head on, or she'd know I was on some bullshit. Trying to appeal to her as a gold digger didn't seem like the right way though. If that was the case, she would've jumped at the chance to be with me or Flex regardless of how I'd acted. Then again, she could've been a hoe with standards and wasn't willing to get treated like shit just for some money.

I'd watched her videos and still didn't really know shit about her besides that she loved her kid and had a few hustles, but she could've been telling them hoes anything for a follow. Obviously, trying to figure her out indirectly wasn't working, but since she had been damn near attached to Yara's hip lately, maybe she could clue me in. At least that's what I was thinking when I pulled up to my brother's crib. I let myself in like I always did.

"Yoooo, where y'all niggas at!" I shouted, making my voice echo off the walls of the huge foyer, and Yara immediately popped out of her little beauty room with one of those bald ass caps on her head.

"Nigga, didn't I tell you to stop coming in here yellin'!"

"Ain't you yellin' too?" I teased, blocking the slap she tried to land as I inspected the top of her head.

"I'm only yellin' 'cause you yellin', punk." She lowered her voice and jumped at me again. "I swear you get on my nerves." She was already heading back to the room she'd come out of, and I trailed behind her.

"Yo, my niece and nephew don't be confused when they see yo' ass lookin' like a conehead with that shit on?" I asked, only half joking. She side eyed me but was unable to stop her laughter from bubbling out.

"Fuck you." She ducked into her room and I was shocked to

see Amari when I stepped in behind her. Just like the last time I'd come while she was doing Yara's hair, she stayed over by the vanity staring daggers at me, but instead of ignoring her like before, I took the time to really take her in. Dressed in a crop top and some baggy cargo jeans, she looked effortlessly cute, especially since her face was bare of makeup. Her hair was in a high messy bun and it flopped around whenever she moved her head, which was often since she kept trying to busy herself, but I kept catching her eyes on me.

"Aye, you got one of them things on under yo' hair too?" I cocked my head as I asked, and she looked like she'd swallowed her tongue then narrowed her eyes on me again.

"Don't worry about it," she quipped dryly, and Yara, who'd been checking on the baby, shoved me before walking back over to her chair.

"Shit, I'm just askin'."

"Well don't." She focused back on Yara's head, her tone flat as hell, and I realized I'd really turned her off me. That just meant I'd have to work even harder to get on her good side. This shit was really turning into more work than I'd planned.

"Leave her alone, Psalm," Yara's big-headed ass interjected while I peeked over into Coco's playpen.

"Ain't nobody thinkin' 'bout y'all, I was just tryna see somethin'," I lied. "Where the boys at though?" My question had Amari's eyes flickering my way briefly, before she dropped them back to her work.

"They're taking a nap, and you bet not go in there and wake them up either!" Yara was quick to say, looking like she'd beat my ass if I even thought about fucking with them. My face balled up and I checked the time on my watch.

"Nigga, it's two in the afternoon! Fuck you do, drug they lil' asses? I know damn well they ain't all sleep at the same time." I looked down at Coco a little harder, like I was really worried, before looking at Yara with accusing eyes.

"They went to the park earlier, goofy! They played until they were tired!" she huffed, getting fed up with me. "Ugh, go bother your brother or something!"

"He here?" I was surprised because he was hardly ever home, which was why I came over so often just to make sure Yara and the kids were straight. He'd told me he was done fucking with Koi's weird ass, and I hadn't really believed him, but maybe he was trying to leave her alone. When Yara confirmed that he was in the theater, I went looking for him.

"Broooo!" I called when I entered the room and saw Saint's big ass lounging in his robe and slippers with a bowl of popcorn in his lap.

"What's up, bro?" He slapped hands with me as I reached him and dropped into the chair next to him.

"Shit, just stopping through to see what y'all on." I shrugged, getting comfortable. "What yo' domesticated ass doin'?"

"Ahhhh, you got jokes." He mugged me before turning back to the movie screen where *Harlem Nights* was playing.

"Nah, I'ma stop playing with you. You gone be in the crib all day?" I wondered, and he nodded, stuffing a handful of popcorn in his mouth with his greedy ass.

"Yea, just waiting on Yara to finish and bring her ass up here," he said like it wasn't that big of a deal, but I was proud of him.

"That's a good look." I dapped him, not wanting to do too much, but it was definitely a win in my book. "I need you to do me a favor though."

"I shouldn't do shit after you threatened to snitch on me," he complained, looking back at the screen. I ignored the soft shit he was on because I wasn't even being for real when I'd said that shit and he knew it. Snitching on him would be like snitching on myself since I obviously knew what he was doing. Angel's ass wasn't about to fuck me up 'cause of his bullshit! Hell no!

"Anyway, when Yara finish, try to keep her busy so I can drive shorty home." He turned my way slowly with a big ass grin on his face.

"You tryna get at Amari?"

"Naw, I'm tryna get at Malice," I corrected and went through the story of how I'd found out she was his baby mama. By the time I finished, he'd agreed to distract Yara for me, and we spent the next hour or so talking about the company and our artists' releases. The whole time he was texting Yara to find out how close they were to being done. When she finally let him know she was finished, he told her to come up there so he could see how good she looked.

Like clockwork, she busted in the theater room a few minutes later with a blonde wig on. I took that as my cue to go catch up with Amari, and when I made it downstairs, she was still packing her little bag up. With my hands in my pockets, I stepped in, clearing my throat for her attention.

"You ready to go?" I tried to sound dry as fuck about having to take her home, and either my tone or having to ride with me had her looking my way annoyed.

"Yara's taking me home." Shaking my head, I motioned upstairs.

"Nah, I don't think she bouta go nowhere for a minute," I hinted to her, but she didn't seem to catch on to what I was saying.

Her perfectly arched brows scrunched together and she tilted her head at me irritably. "What? Matter fact, nevermind, I'll just wait or get a Uber." She went right back to packing her stuff, and I had to stop myself from snapping on her.

"I got something to do over that way so you might as well come now since you're almost done in here," I said smartly, and before she could try to argue, I added, "I'll go grab Prince." I could see her mind working, trying to process a response, but I went in search of her shorty without giving her a chance to. I found him and Saint in the playroom laid out in sleeping bags, and I shook my head. Them niggas had to have been all over the damn park to still be napping, but that was even better for me. It'd give me time to talk to Amari without having to censor shit.

I picked him up with ease and made my way out to my truck,

buckling him into the backseat before getting behind the wheel. As soon as I started it up, the radio came on loud as hell and I hurried to cut it down so it wouldn't disturb him. He was still knocked out and drooling on the little jersey he wore. Minutes passed, and it seemed like Amari's ass wasn't about to come out for a second, but she eventually did with attitude all over her pretty face. She had probably planned on not leaving until she saw that I really had taken her son to the car.

She barely looked at me as she tossed her bag inside and got in herself, checking to make sure Prince was good.

"Man, he straight," I told her when she still hadn't turned back around. I had a feeling she was inspecting the way I'd put the seatbelt on him, with her extra ass. "I do got a niece and nephew, so I know how to strap a kid in, but they got car seats though," I admonished, and her neck snapped in my direction. Sucking her teeth, she sat straight and roughly pulled on her seatbelt as I drove off. If her shorty hadn't been in the car, I would've sped out and slammed on the brake to jerk her goofy ass.

"For your information, he does have a car seat it's just in my mama's car," she sneered, rolling her neck and shit.

"You gone have to calm all that spicy shit down. I was just sayin', I know how to hook kids up in car seats."

"That's not what it sounded like," she shot back. "It sounded like you were tryna say he doesn't have a car seat or something. So I was just letting you know he does... it's just in my mama's car 'cause I'm not carrying that big ass thing around."

"Why don't his daddy help you carry it? He got one of those too, right?" I already knew I was about to catch hell behind that shit, and when her head snapped in my direction, she was giving me a look that could kill.

"What the fuck is your problem with me? Like, do you wanna fight or something? 'Cause you seem like you got smoke with me and I'm just tryna figure this shit out." She had the nerve to ball her little fists up as she turned almost completely in her seat.

The fact that she even thought to say some shit like that had me laughing as I looked between her and the road. "Yo, you tweakin'! What the fuck makes you think I'd fight yo' ass?"

"'Cause ever since I met yo' black ass you either lookin' at me crazy or sayin' something crazy, so you must want an issue." The seriousness in her tone had me wondering if she'd really fought a nigga before because she was just acting too tough. She had to be mad as hell though, so I needed to calm her ass down before she did some silly shit and hit me.

Sighing, I stroked my beard. "I ain't got an issue with you. I'ma keep it real and let you know I don't like the company you keep. Ole girl really ain't a good look for you."

"Who, Koi?"

I resisted the urge to call her a bitch as I nodded. "Yeah, her ass." She did that little tongue clicking thing women did but finally straightened up in her seat.

"Look, I don't have shit to do with what Koi and your brother got going on. I didn't even know Saint was the nigga she was messing with until that night at the club."

"But you know now, and you don't think it's fucked up to be friends with her and Yara?" That was something I actually did want to know. I fucked with sis, and I didn't want anybody around that had ill intentions for her.

"It's not like I condone the shit Koi's doing. I let her know that shit was messy, especially because I've been following Yara for a while and she knows that. It was like a personal goal for me to get on Yara's level when it comes to this influencer thing, so when we met and she wanted to work with me, I wasn't trying to pass that up. Especially because of Koi's bullshit. Is it fucked up? Yeah, but I'm not telling Yara about that shit for the same reason you haven't. It's not my place to tell and I'm not tryna hurt her either." Silence filled the car as I considered what she'd said, and I couldn't help but agree with her. Nodding with a shrug, I pulled up to her crib.

"I'll give you that. It was fucked up to judge you based off what your friend be on, especially since you wasn't on that with me 'cause of my brother. So my bad…truce?" She paused for a few seconds, studying me like she was trying to see how serious I was before she sighed.

"Okay, truce." She finally gave a small grin and then moved to get out, but I stopped her.

"So, since we got off on a bad note, let me get a do-over?"

"I am not goin' on a date with you." She chuckled, shaking her head, and I drew back in exaggerated offense.

"Who said shit about a date? We're friends now, right? Ain't shit wrong with two friends hanging out. I'll even let you pick where we go." I tried to sweeten the deal, but she looked like she was about to deny me again. "I mean, technically, we've already kicked it twice, so at least the next time, it can be doing something fun that doesn't involve being in my car."

She tilted her head cutely like she was considering and then swiftly shot me down. "I'll think about it." She was out the car, getting Prince out before I could come back with something. "Bye, *friend*." She cheesed, slamming the back door shut quickly.

"Fuck!" I grumbled, watching her go into her apartment. She probably thought she was off the hook, but I wasn't giving up that easy.

Koi

I blinked back tears and tried not to scream as another one of my calls to Saint went to voicemail. It had been a whole week since I'd talked to him, and either he'd blocked me, or he was ignoring all my calls still. Whatever it was, it was getting on my last nerve. He had me out here looking like Amari's soft ass, and she was the last bitch I was trying to be like. I didn't cry over niggas and I damn sure didn't stalk their phones. When things inevitably ended, I was the one that was ignoring their calls, but for some reason, shit with Saint was different. I didn't know if it was because he'd broken up with me or if it was actual love I felt, but either way, I didn't like it. I'd found myself watching his social media and even Yara's on a daily basis, and that was a big mistake. Not only was that nigga really pretending they were one big happy family, but Amari's traitor ass was often on Yara's page like they were the best of friends. That really burned me up because she wouldn't have even known them if it wasn't for me.

This whole time I'd been expecting her to apologize to me for the shit she'd said at her house, but I guess she was too busy being up Yara's ass. She had gained a lot more followers and her videos were blowing up now that she'd linked up with Yara. I would've gotten her more if I had made videos with her like she'd begged me to all those times, but I'd let her think she was doing something with her phony ass.

"Okay, I'm all done," Sonia, my hairstylist, said as she smoothed my side-swooped ponytail down. I looked up from my phone and checked her work in the mirror, shooing her hands away so I could see better. It was exactly like the picture I'd shown her, even down to the baby hairs. She was lucky too, because if it hadn't been, then her ass wasn't going to get paid. Satisfied, I sent over her money on CashApp like I always did and even added a couple dollars since she'd done such a good job.

"Thanks, girl! I'm gone!" I shouted over my shoulder as I made my way to her door in a hurry.

"Hold up, Koi girl, I think your app made a mistake or something. You were like twenty bucks short." Sonia rushed up behind me, and I rolled my eyes.

"That's 'cause this swoop and these baby hairs are short! If you would've done it like the picture I showed you then I would've paid you the whole amount!" I watched her face contort as she tried to figure out a peaceful way to respond, but if she thought she was getting the last twenty, she was highly mistaken.

"You know I did that shit just like the pictures—"

"Girl, boom! If I was trying to stiff you for a lil' measly ass dub, I could've just let my friend Amari do it for free! Matter fact, let me just go live so we can see what TikTok thinks then! I bet you they see the same shit I see and yo' ass gone be canceled just like that!" I snapped my fingers for emphasis and she followed the movement with a red face. Nobody wanted to get their business fucked with by them crazy motherfuckers on TikTok. Knowing that, she sucked her teeth, waving for me to go ahead, and I smiled widely.

It wasn't that I didn't have the money, but if I could get something done for a lower price, then I would. Fuck what she was talking about. I switched out of her suite and to my car, feeling good until my phone buzzed with a call from my baby daddy. I started not to answer because he had Blaze and I didn't want to seem available if he wanted me to get her. There was an influencer party going on and I wasn't trying to miss that, especially if there was a chance that Saint was there on Yara's arm. I thought I was left off the hook when the call ended up going to voicemail, but his ass called right back, and I rolled my eyes as I climbed into my car and answered.

"What do you want, Dolavan! I'm busy!" I shouted, calling him by his stupid ass first name.

"Aye, watch how the fuck you talk to me, bro." I could tell he was mugging me through the phone and even though I was talking shit in my head, I answered him in a much less aggressive voice.

"My bad Dola, what is it? I hope you don't want me to get Blaze 'cause I'm on my way inside of the influencer party." I was talking fast, hoping it would make him feel rushed.

"When do I ever give a fuck about what you got goin' on when I have my baby, Koi? Don't piss me off, bro. I'm callin' yo' simple ass 'cause I wanna know if I can keep her for another week. I got a show out in Florida and I wanna take her to Disneyland."

"Wait, if you gone be at a show then who gone have my baby?" I asked just to seem like I gave a fuck when I was going to give him the okay to take her regardless. An extra week without having to worry about her was exactly what I needed while I dealt with this Saint drama.

"The same nanny I always have get her, goofy!" He was already huffing and puffing into the phone, and I rolled my eyes at the unnecessary aggression but didn't move to check him. I liked to let Amari think that I still had Dola wrapped around my finger, but the truth was he couldn't stand my ass, and the only reason he was cordial was because of Blaze. I was actually lucky because Malik didn't like Amari either, but he did her dirty every chance he got to the point I was convinced he hated Prince too.

"Well damn, you don't have to get all mad. I was just asking, just make sure your child support—" The phone beeped in my ear, letting me know he'd hung up, and I sucked my teeth.

Whether he answered me or not, I knew my account better had been a few thousand bigger by the weekend. Tossing my phone on the passenger seat, I pulled off, headed for the party. I was already running late because of Sonia and Dola's asses, but at least I'd get more attention coming in that way. The white, printed Chanel tennis jumpsuit I was wearing with the shoes to match was definitely an eye catcher, and all a bitch needed was a tennis racket. I rapped along to Cardi B as I zipped through traffic and when I finally pulled up, I grinned widely at the amount of cameras outside.

I brought the car to a stop and a valet immediately came over to give me a ticket and take the keys to my Lexus. The paid bodyguards escorted me to the red carpet and cameras were flashing all over. I struck a couple of poses so they could catch my dress from different angles before one of the organizers led me inside. The space was decorated from corner to corner with black and gold balloons and glitter. Champagne flutes were everywhere, and I realized it was because there was a champagne fountain in the center of the room that was so huge we would be drinking from it for days. I immediately headed over to it, bypassing the table of food and the loud ass DJ booth. I grabbed a healthy glass and started sipping it as I watched the crowd to see who was there and who wasn't. Two sweeps and there was no sign of Yara, but I did end up making eye contact with a messy ass wig influencer named Miles. As soon as our eyes locked, he pursed his glossy lips and switched over to me, looking tacky as fuck with a glass of champagne in each hand. I groaned inwardly and tried to look for an escape before he got too close, but there wasn't enough people there for me to disappear into a crowd.

"Heeeeeeey, Koi! Don't you look cute!" he gushed over my outfit with a nod of approval, but I didn't give him the same energy back even though I did like the way he fit into his salmon-colored polo shirt and shorts. If he wasn't gay, people probably would've thought we came together since we both looked country club ready.

"Thank youuu!" I faked enthusiasm and returned the air kisses he gave me.

"Oh shit, here we go," he said, looking behind me at the sudden commotion I heard. When I turned around, my nose instantly turned up at the sight of Yara walking in with Amari right next to her. I damn sure hadn't been expecting that or the way everybody was swarming them, from the camera crews to the guests. Before I could clock their outfits, the crowd blocked them, and I instantly wanted to scream. "Ugh, I should've known she was going to bring that damn new girl! Her ass ain't been an influencer but two minutes and now she coming to parties and stealing folks brand deals," he complained so only I could hear, and I damn near spit out my champagne.

"Brand deals! Like as in plural!" My eyes shot back to Amari since the crowd of people had moved away, and I immediately got irritated seeing she was wearing another Shein outfit. How the fuck was anybody reaching out to her to promote them and she was spending less than five dollars on her outfits? I wanted to be able to say that Yara had set her up for the okiedoke so I could throw that shit in her face, but I could tell from where I was standing that she was also wearing something from the site too.

"Yeah girl, Pluto and So Nice wigs." Miles tsked, shaking his head, and I gasped. I'd seen that on her video with Yara she was thanking all her new followers, but she hadn't said anything about brand deals! It was no way she'd gotten that much attention just from doing a dusty ass wig on Yara! Suddenly, I had a headache just thinking about that shit, but seeing Saint walk in behind them really had me fucked up. I watched as he wrapped his arms around Yara for a few pictures, and the smile on his face made me sick to my stomach. Not too long ago he was holding me like that and letting me take pictures of us whenever I wanted. Hell, if anybody looked at my camera roll they'd think I was that nigga's fiancée and not just the bitch he was fucking! I was so busy shooting daggers their way that I was no longer listening to shit Miles was saying. It took everything in me not to throw that champagne glass into the fountain and knock every bit of food off the serving table. Saint really had me ready to crash out. Like I really wanted to walk over and snatch him away, because who the fuck was she? I'd been the one that he was spending most of his nights with, and to all of a sudden be cut off just so he could be with her was crazy. What made it all worse was that I couldn't even say Yara was ugly, or fat, or a hoe, because none of that was true. Even after having their baby she was still fit and had even gotten thicker in all the right places. I wasn't used to feeling envious of anybody, but I swear I wanted everything Yara had... well, except for the kids. She could keep those little fuckers because I barely even wanted my own kid. There was no way I'd take on her little brats.

"Koi! Koi, girl, you okay?" Miles' annoying voice interrupted my thoughts, and I tried to shake off the silent rage I was feeling.

Forcing my eyes from the couple, I bit my jaw to keep from telling him to get the fuck out my face. "Yeah, I just zoned out for a minute. I'm cool," I lied and quickly emptied my glass, ready for another one.

"Oh shit! Don't look now, but they're coming this waaaaay!" I barely had time to prepare before Amari and Yara were in my face with an uncomfortable-looking Saint. "Heeeey, boo!" Miles' fake ass cooed, giving Yara the same air kiss he'd given me like he wasn't just talking shit about them both.

"How you doin', Miles? I don't know if y'all have met, but this is Amari. She's been doing big things!" My face twitched listening to her gloat about *my* best friend, but I tuned them out as my eyes shifted to Saint. He was looking so good I would've sucked his dick right then in front of everybody, his bitch included. I knew he could feel the hole I was staring in the side of his face, but he was going out of his way to look at everything but me. If he thought I was going to let him play in my face though, he had me fucked up.

"Hey, Saint!" My voice came out high pitched even though I'd meant to sound normal. Instantly, it seemed like the air was sucked from the room and the conversation around us ceased. From the corner of my eye, I could see Amari's stupid ass with her mouth dropped open, but I was too focused on Saint to give a fuck. His jaw clenched as he finally turned my way with a silent warning in his eyes.

"What's up, Koi? You talked to Flex today?" he hinted, and I felt my nose turn up at him asking me about Flex's bum ass. His eyes shifted to Yara, who was watching us closely, and I finally caught on.

"Oh, not since earlier." An awkward chuckle bubbled up in my throat. "He was supposed to be meeting me here," I lied and waited to see if Saint had any reaction, but of course, he didn't give a damn because he'd set up that lie.

"Cool, I'll run into him," he said, barely looking at me. Seemingly done with the conversation, he leaned down into Yara's ear. "How long we gotta stay here, babe? I'm tryna get you up outta this shit." I assumed none of us were supposed to hear that, and he was just a shitty-ass whisperer, but a big part of me felt like he'd said it loud enough for me to hear on purpose. It seemed like he was playing in my face, and he had me fucked up.

"Saaaaint, I brought Amari with me to network," Yara giggled, and I wanted to throw up. "Let me introduce her to a few people and then we can go. Come on, boo, let's go work the room a little before this nigga loses his mind."

"I'ma catch up with you," Amari said, and Yara walked off with Saint. I swear if looks could kill, Yara's ass would've been on the ground bloody. I was still staring after them when Amari excused us from Miles and guided me a few feet away. "Bitch, what the fuck is wrong with you? Why would you do that?" she hissed as soon as we were far enough away, and I rolled my eyes at her dramatic ass.

"Girl, please, she wasn't paying me any attention. She go out of her way not to see the shit he do. Why the fuck do you even care anyway? You're *my* best friend, so what you worried about that bitch for? Oh, that's right, you're on her dick 'cause she put you on, right?" I chuckled bitterly, annoyed that she was even trying to check me about Yara's ass.

"You keep saying shit about Yara, but you're the same friend that I asked for a plug time and time again, and you always had some type of excuse not to get on camera, but you'd let me do your hair, makeup, and nails for free any other time. I ain't known that girl a whole month and she was more than happy to share her spotlight with me, and she pays me every time I do a service for her, unlike my *best friend* or my weak ass baby daddy. But you know what, I'm not even bouta argue with yo' crazy ass! You want her to find out, cool, but I hope you're prepared for him not to be with you if she leaves him." She'd quickly read me for filth and switched off before I could even come up with a response. *Bitch!*

An hour later, I was at my table watching Saint and that bitch's every move as they worked the room either together or separately. Most of the time he was glued to her hip like he was afraid I'd corner her and blow up his spot, but I had something more beneficial in mind. I'd watched Saint throwing back glass after glass of the expensive champagne and it was only a matter of time before he had to go to the bathroom. As if God was listening, right then Saint whispered something in Yara's ear and started walking to the hallway where the bathrooms were. I was so thirsty, I wasn't even trying to be discreet as I jumped up and followed him. I quickly checked to make sure nobody was watching before going down that same hallway and into the men's bathroom. Saint was already standing at the urinal peeing, and my heart pounded as I locked the door, instantly drawing his attention.

He instantly shook his head at the sight of me and groaned. "Man, get yo' ass outta here, Koi." He seemed more annoyed than angry, so I ignored that shit and kept walking to him.

"Not until you give me what I want," I pouted, sliding my panties down my thighs without taking my eyes off him. "I ain't had no dick in days, and I'm so fuckin' wet right now." His eyes dropped to the wetness that had reached my thighs and I saw the internal battle there. *I knew he still wanted me!* By now, he'd stopped peeing and his dick was already coming to life.

"Fuck, Koi!" he moaned lowly as I reached him. "I told you I can't do this shit no more."

"*Please.*" I stood on my toes and kissed him, sucking his bottom lip in my mouth. "I *need* you," I whimpered, rubbing my wetness on his dick, and I grinned triumphantly when he lifted me in his arms with a growl.

Wrapping my legs around him as he carried me over to the sink, I slipped my tongue in his mouth, getting excited. My insides quaked from the anticipation and just knowing that Yara wasn't too far away.

"Hurry uuuup! I need to feel you!" I pressed, getting annoyed when he took the time to retrieve a condom out of his wallet. I didn't want to turn him off by nagging about why he wouldn't just go in without it, so I kept my irritation to myself and felt like shouting when he'd finally pulled it on. "Ahhhh!" a satisfied sigh came out when he slipped inside me, filling me up completely. He paused for a few seconds, resting his forehead against mine, and I was almost salivating by now. Finding his lips again, I winded my hips until he slid out and then thrust back into me with enough force that I cried out.

Boom! Boom! Boom!

"Hey, is anybody in there?" somebody shouted as they beat on the bathroom door. Saint instantly stilled and tried to pull out, but I squeezed my legs around him tighter.

"Noooo, baby, don't stop!" I was still trying to lure his attention from the door, but whoever was out there was relentless. Once we heard them talking to somebody else about going to get a key, Saint wrestled away, looking like he wanted to slap the shit out of me. We sat there panting and glaring at each other for a second before the sound of a loud-ass maintenance man had him quickly pulling up his jeans.

"Get in the fuckin' closet!" he ordered, but I looked at him like he was stupid.

"Are you gonna stop this dumb shit and come over tonight?" I was acting like I had all the time in the world, but I wasn't about to let him wiggle out of this one.

"Yeah, man!" he hissed, snatching me down from the sink. I didn't even care about his attitude. I happily snatched up my panties.

"I'm not going in that dirty ass closet though. This is a white Chanel dress." I cocked my head at him when he acted like he wanted to argue. When he finally let me go, I went to the last stall and locked it before carefully standing on the toilet. I listened silently as Saint opened the door and pretended to be pissed off because he'd been stuck. His voice faded and the nigga that had been trying to get in did his business and left. Once he was gone, I waited another minute or so before I left out and damn near skipped across to the women's room to clean up for the drive home. I no longer gave a damn about this party, Yara, or even Amari's ass. I had my nigga back!

Yara

I sat in the passenger seat and eyed Saint as he drove home in silence. His whole vibe had been off ever since we'd left the party and I had no clue why. I thought we were having a good time. Hell, I was sure we were, up until he came back from the bathroom ready to go. At first, I thought it was because he was trying to get me home like he'd said, but the attitude radiating off of him said otherwise. I caught on real fucking quick when his response to anything I asked him was met with a dry ass response. Even Amari was uncomfortable, and I felt bad as hell because I was the one who'd invited her only to make her leave early and deal with whatever Saint had going on.

Since we were finally alone, I decided to try my hand with him again. "So, do you wanna tell me what's wrong since we're by ourselves now?" I asked, trying to interlock our fingers, but he immediately pulled away and put his hand on the steering wheel. It was shit like this that made me want to just say fuck it. We'd be good for a little bit of time and then he'd randomly feel like being a dick for no reason. It had to be a mental illness because the shit wasn't normal behavior, and I didn't deserve to be on the receiving end of his moodiness.

"My bad bae, my shit asleep, and it helps when I hold on to

the steering wheel," he lied, sounding stupid as hell. I hadn't ever heard him say no shit like that in all the years we'd been together. He hadn't even tried when he pulled that lie out his ass, and it took the strength of God not to make me go upside his head.

"Oh damn, I forgot your hand randomly falls asleep and only the steering wheel makes it better." My sarcasm had him blowing out a heavy breath, and I knew exactly what was coming. Gaslighting. The shit was like clockwork, and the fact that I was becoming so used to it that I could see the signs was telling as fuck.

"Bro, you act like you ain't ever heard of carpal tunnel! Fuck would I need to lie about some shit like that for?"

"Shit, you tell me!" I fumed, getting even more angry that he'd done exactly what I knew he would. "Just an hour ago, you were all up on me, and now I can't even touch yo' fuckin' hand! So tell me what happened between then and now that got yo' goofy ass lying about carpal tunnel! Carpal fuckin' tunnel! Nigga, you don't even do shit that would give you carpal tunnel!"

"I can't fuckin' talk to you, bro. You always think I'm lying about some shit!"

"'Cause you always lying!" I screamed, realizing that I was wasting my time. Taking a deep breath, I closed my eyes and tried to calm down. "You know what, I'm not gone argue with you, Saint. If you claim you got carpal tunnel, then that's what you got."

"Yara—"

"We're good, Saint," I cut him off and prayed he'd just take the easy way out and leave me alone. I was liable to lose the battle I was having with myself and fuck him up. God was on my side because he stayed quiet, probably reflecting on how dumb he sounded.

I was so grateful when he pulled into our circular drive that I was pulling my seatbelt off and reaching for the handle before he could come to a full stop. As soon as my feet touched the ground, I was damn near running in the house to get away from him. Shit,

I wished I could lock him out the house, but that would be childish. *It was childish to lie about carpal tunnel and that didn't stop his ass!*

"Yara!" I cursed under my breath when he came in the door behind me. I was hoping he'd just leave like he normally did when we fell out. *It was probably too early in the day for him*, I thought snidely, taking off my heels as I ascended our stairs. "Fuck is you being stupid for? I'm tryna talk to you!" Saint continued to yell like he didn't know I was actively ignoring him. By the time I'd reached our bedroom, he'd caught up to me and grabbed my arm.

"What!"

"I'm trying to apologize, Ya. You're right, I shouldn't have moved my hand away." His voice was much calmer than it'd been this whole time and I couldn't do shit but laugh.

"Thank you," I quipped, tilting my head up at him. "Is that all you'd like to say?"

Confused, he studied me for a few seconds before realization came over his face. "Stop doin' that passive-aggressive shit, Ya! I apologized!"

"Oooh, passive aggressive, that's such a big word for Elmo!"

"Bro—"

"Look, you apologized, and I said thank you. I really don't know what else you want now, Saint. I'm good." I smiled, only making him more uneasy. "Do you wanna order out for dinner or should I cook?"

"Man, fuck you, bro!" he grumbled, storming off. I waited until I heard the front door slam before continuing into my bedroom and undressing for a bath. I was so glad my parents had the kids. It would give me a few hours alone to clear my mind because I really needed to figure out if my relationship was worth saving.

The next morning, I woke up to a dozen red roses on Saint's pillow and rolled my eyes. I liked flowers just like the next girl, but if he thought that weak ass apology and some flowers were going to get him back on my good side, he was dumber than he looked. Groaning, I knocked them bitches on the floor and turned over, but a sea of red caught my eyes before I could close them good. I shot straight up, stunned by the sea of roses covering my floor. Our bedroom was damn near four hundred square feet and every inch of it besides a path to the bathroom and one to our room door was covered in red eternal roses. While it surprised me and was gorgeous, it was just another part of our cycle, and this time I didn't know if I could go through it with him.

I knew Saint was lying about that carpal tunnel shit, and the fact that he'd done so over something so insignificant was what really fucked me up. How could I marry a nigga that lied about shit like that? One who couldn't even give me peace for more than a week before he hit me with another personality.

Sighing, I climbed out of bed and went to handle my hygiene. After taking a shower, I slipped on a comfortable Ethika two piece and headed downstairs. As soon as I came out of the room I could smell breakfast being cooked and realized that Saint was still home. That was good because I needed him to get all those damn flowers. However, when I entered the kitchen, it was Saint's mom Angel cooking. Frowning, I looked around like he'd pop out, but her laughter stopped me.

"Girl, Saint is not here." She pushed a plate onto the island and motioned for me to sit down. I did so slowly and my mouth watered at the plate of pancakes, eggs, and bacon. "Yeah, his scary ass left before you could wake up," she explained, making me groan.

"Great, so now I gotta clean that mess up." I roughly cut into my pancakes and added syrup.

"The roses?" she asked, wincing, and I nodded. It was way too many for me to be able to gather them all up. That shit would take all day and I didn't have time for that, not to mention where would I put all of them. I'd really have to order some kind of truck and have them donated maybe. It was irresponsible of Saint to get that shit, and now I'd be stuck figuring out how to clear my bedroom of them while he was just gone. "Well, that's not good."

"What?" I wanted to know, pausing as I held my fork up.

"Baby, your man left you a room full of very beautiful and very expensive roses and your immediate thought is that it's a mess you gotta clean up?" She raised her brow at me, but I was still lost. My confusion must have been clear because she set her mug down and planted her arms on the island. "Yara, a gift shouldn't be considered a mess, girl. If anything, seeing those roses when you woke up should've had you all over your man. Who cares about them being all over the floor? Your man spent a bag just so you could wake up in your own botanical garden and you found something wrong with it." I slumped on my chair as her words sank in.

"Well damn, when you put it like that."

Angel leaned over and touched my hand with a sympathetic look. "You've checked out, honey. You add life, kids, and a nigga that keeps fucking up, and well, it happens, but that's when you have to put the spice back in your life. Shake shit up and make it exciting again." A smile came over her face like she was having thoughts about her own life. It wasn't as simple as she was making it seem though. Spice wasn't our issue. Saint's lying about little things was though.

I could already feel the tears coming on, and I blinked to try and keep them from falling. "It's more than just that though. Saint's been lying about the dumbest shit and being super... sketchy, and not to mention randomly disappearing—"

"Oh, that's easy. That nigga cheatin'." She shrugged like she hadn't just accused her son of messing around on me, and I gasped.

"*Angel*, really?"

"Look, that's my son and I love him to death, but those ingredients you just mixed up equal to a cheating nigga pie. I know it and you might be in denial, but you know it too. I'm just trying to figure out why you haven't left his ass yet." She tilted her head like she was waiting for an actual answer while I was still trying to gather my thoughts. Everything she'd said made so much sense that I felt like a fool. All the times I'd caught him in lies, the random late nights, and his weird behavior were all signs, and I'd avoided them like they weren't right in my face.

"Damn, I-I guess I don't know," I stuttered, looking around like I'd find the answer somewhere in the kitchen.

"I think you do know. Shit, every woman knows, especially when she's in love, but love will have you fucked up if you let it. Men will have you fucked up in general, hell." We both laughed. "After dealing with the boys' father, I promised myself that if I was ever in a situation like this with one of their girlfriends or wives, I wouldn't be the mama that condoned her son's shit. What y'all call it now, a girl's girl? That's what I'm trying to be right now when I say that if that nigga is out here risking y'all relationship, then you need to do what's best for you." She gave me a pointed look before moving to collect the dishes she'd used for washing, and I silently went back to my food. She'd given me a lot to think about, and what scared me the most was that I kind of already knew what I needed to do.

SAINT

I'd been checking my phone waiting on a word from my OG or Yara's ass, but I wasn't getting shit but radio silence. It had been hours since I'd had those roses set up in our bedroom for her, and I knew she was woke by now. I'd even had my mama over there to have breakfast with her and talk on my behalf. I expected something by now, and the longer I went without hearing from either of them the more stressed out I was getting.

When my phone rang and I saw my mama's name, I damn near broke my finger to answer. "Damn Ma, what took you so long?"

"First of all, watch yo' mouth nigga, and second of all, don't rush me! I did you a favor!" she huffed, and I could hear her light up a cigarette.

"My bad, Ma, but damn, you been MIA! I'm just tryna see if it's safe for me to go home. Like, is she cool? Did she like the roses? What she say?" I hurried to close my office door so nobody could hear me in there sounding like a simp. I was so damn nervous my hands were clammy, and I wiped them on my jeans as I waited for her to answer.

"Fuck all that! Why didn't you tell me you were out here

cheating on that girl?" she caught me off guard by saying. I'd been about to drop back into my swivel chair, but I instantly began pacing.

"Who told you that? Is that what she said?" I'd been paranoid as fuck since that shit with Koi in the bathroom, and it was even worse now since I hadn't gone to her house like I said I would. My first thought was that she'd contacted Yara and snitched on me, and I didn't know if I'd be able to control myself if she had.

My mama blew smoke into the phone and smacked her lips. "You nigga, the shit you doin' is what told me that! Yara ain't have to say shit," she huffed angrily, and I let out a sigh of relief. "You just like yo' damn daddy! Can't do right for shit!"

"Ma, man, ain't nobody cheatin' on Yara—"

"So you ain't out here lying and being sneaky?" she cut me off with an attitude and before I could lie, she was shooting out another question. "You not being all moody and hot and cold? You definitely out here cheating, and I told Yara if she was smart, she'd leave yo' ass and take the ring."

"**YOU TOLD HER WHAT!**" I exploded, ready to crash the fuck out. "Why the fuck would you tell her that!"

"I told her to do what was best for her, and if that's leaving yo' cheating ass then hey—" She was still talking when I hung up on her. No wonder Yara wasn't calling me and shit! The muthafucka I'd sent to help the situation only added fuel to the fire and suggested she leave me! Yara and my mama had a good enough relationship that she'd take her advice and do that shit without question.

Snatching my keys up from my desk, I dialed her number and was met with the voicemail, but I continued calling as I left my office in a rush. By the time I made it to my car and pulled off, the shit was going straight to voicemail and I knew right then she'd blocked me. That had me violating traffic laws and risking my life to get home. It took damn near an hour with afternoon traffic, but when I finally pulled up I was relieved to see Yara's BMW still there. I left the car running and ran inside with my heart beating out of my chest.

"Yara! Yara!" I started up the stairs, thinking I'd find her there, but she came from the direction of her beauty room, carrying a couple makeup bags in her hands. "Baby!" I ignored the look of unease on her face and made my way over until she was within arm's reach.

Tears glistened in her eyes and she backed away from me. "I...I can't do this with you right now," she said lowly, and my eyes narrowed. The way she was clutching her makeup cases and the way her gaze was all shifty had me following her line of sight to her luggage. Even SJ and Coco's bags were stacked up neatly next to hers. The relief I'd been feeling evaporated, and I glared at her suspiciously.

"You bouta leave me, Yara?" I asked, pissed at how shook up she seemed even though I'd never laid a hand on her. She'd let my mama fuck with her head and now she thought I was an abusive ass cheater. "You fuckin' leavin' over that shit yesterday!"

"No, I'm leavin' over a bunch of shit." Her voice trembled slightly, but she didn't back down. "Yesterday just happened to be the latest thing."

"What you want me to do, baby? Just tell me, I'll do whatever you want." I was begging and sounding like a straight bitch, but if that's what it took to keep my family intact, then so be it. Judging from the look on her face, I could tell she didn't believe me, but I also had never been so close to losing her before.

"I want you to tell the truth! Is that one of the things you're willing to do?"

That damn sure wasn't what I thought she was going to want from me, and I hesitated to speak too quickly. Sighing, I stroked my beard, and the delay had Yara bucking at me. "What you wanna know, Ya?" I could tell she didn't think I'd be honest, but I wasn't letting her go that easy. She folded her arms and raised a brow.

"Have you cheated?" She looked at me smugly, waiting for me

to either tell on myself or deny everything. I couldn't believe my mama had put me in a situation like this, and now Yara was about to have me confessing over a hunch my OG had. My jaw clenched and I tried to gas myself up to tell her.

"Yeah." Yara's face fell in disappointment. Despite the tough front she tried to put on, my confession had fucked her up. My baby looked crushed and it only made me feel worse about what else I might have to tell her.

"How many times, Saint?" she choked out, hurt evident in her voice. I hated that some shit I'd done was causing her all this hurt. I was trying to stay cool, but the truth was I was going to be at her mercy. I just hoped she'd forgive me.

"Just once. That's it," I vowed, using the opportunity to try to reach for her, but she backed away again.

"Recently?" she wanted to know, and my jaw clenched. It made sense that if she wanted the truth she'd want the type of details only women would think to ask for. I wasn't trying to make shit worse, and I knew certain answers would definitely have her feeling a way, but shit had gone too far to go back now. Reluctantly, I nodded, confirming that the cheating was recent.

"Look, it didn't mean shit, babe. I love *you*, I just—"

Yara put up her hand to stop me. "So who was it? Do I know them?" That shit had me stuck. I'd told her I was going to tell the truth, but if she knew that Koi was the bitch I'd been messing with, she'd fuck around and kill both of us. "It was somebody I know? What the fuck, Saint! You probably got me out here lookin' stupid as fuck! Who is it! Huh! Who is it!" She rushed me and all I could do was wrap my arms around her to keep her from fucking me up. Yara might've been small, but she packed a punch that would leave my ass with a black eye.

"I'm sorry. I'm sorry," I repeated over and over while she cried. I don't know how long we were like that before she suddenly wiggled out of my grip and silently went to gather her things. "Yara—"

"No, fuck you, Saint! You don't love me and you're not sorry either! You're sitting here protecting this bitch? Is it 'cause you love her?" She stopped moving and shot daggers at me.

"What? No! Hell no! I love you, I just—shit, I don't know. I'm a nigga and—" She cut me off with bitter laughter.

"Right, and niggas can't control their dicks! I swear, I can't even look at you right now! All this time you been making me feel stupid! Lying and sneaking around!" Yara tossed her head back with a sniffle, and suddenly her voice was calm again. "Look, I'm gonna go to my parents' until I can find a place for me and the kids. I'll never keep them from you—"

"Yara, bro, you trippin'. This house is for you and the kids. You don't need to take them nowhere. I'll go, y'all stay here." I tried to reason with her, but that just lit the fire back under her ass.

"Why, 'cause you tryna go to that bitch house? Matter fact, have you ever brought her here? Did you fuck that bitch in our bed!"

"Man, hell naw! I'd never bring that bitch here! And this is about my kids being comfortable, it ain't got shit to do with her! Stop fuckin' playin' with me, Ya!"

"Fine then, get the fuck out!" I knew she was really mad because she'd been throwing her makeup bag around and that was some shit she never did. She was always super careful with that shit, so her tossing them around without a care meant she wasn't thinking about shit besides what we were fighting about.

"I gotta get some clothes first Ya, then I'll be out." I kept my voice even, trying to make sure she stayed calm.

"Then me and the kids will come back when you're finished."

"Yara, you don't need to be driving like this—"

"Nigga, fuck you!" she tossed over her shoulder as she stormed out and slammed the door behind her. *Fuck!*

"Man, how long you said you gone need to stay?" Psalm's annoying ass came and sat across from me on the couch. I'd only been there for a half hour and he was already on his bullshit.

"Until I fuckin' feel like it. How 'bout that? This yo' damn mama doin'," I said, grilling him, and he scoffed.

"Then why the fuck you ain't invading her damn guest room?"

The truth was I'd thought about it, but I knew I wasn't going to want to hear her mouth. Besides that, I was still lowkey hot about her putting shit in Yara's head. Was I fucked up for cheating with Koi? Hell yeah. It wasn't like I was doing the shit on purpose though. Koi was just some shit to do. A bitch that paid me the attention I wasn't getting at home since Yara was always so damn focused on the kids or social media. I understood that was her job, but I was also a nigga with needs.

Now I was without my damn family and I didn't even want Koi's attention because she was doing too much. She was making the shit we had going on way more than it was and catching me up, to the point that I was fucking up at home. If I hadn't been worried about Yara killing my ass too, I probably would've told her about Koi, but she was giving off the type of crazy that a simple ass whooping from Yara wouldn't fix.

"I'm tellin' her you was talkin' shit too." Psalm's voice interrupted my thoughts and I mugged him hard.

"And I'm gone tell her that yo' ass was right there with me the whole time, nigga." He feigned shock, and I tossed one of his couch pillows at him, but he blocked it. "You a bitch."

"How yo' ass walkin' around here mad about some shit when it's yo' damn fault? I told you not to keep fuckin' playin' with Yara and you wasn't tryna hear me. You let that crazy bitch rape you in the bathroom and then was around sis without cleaning that bitch off you?" He shook his head with a tsk. "You lucky she don't know that's the real reason y'all got into it yesterday or else she would've been on the news."

I already knew I'd fucked up. I didn't need him adding to it by talking shit. "Fuck you, what was I supposed to do? Get caught in there with that bitch at an influencer party? Them hoes was gone be doing think pieces for weeks if I had! Then Yara definitely wouldn't take me back!"

"Shiiiit, I don't think she gone take you back now, but I get what you sayin'. Ain't nobody tryna get publicly humiliated. Do you think Koi gone stay quiet though?" That was a good question. She'd already threatened me and I hadn't done what she said, so there was no telling what she'd do. With shit so shaky with Yara though, I didn't want to take a chance on going over to her house and getting her crazy ass even more riled up. Shrugging, I scrubbed a hand down my face.

"I hope so. I'm not really tryna fuck with her right now." I lifted my half-empty beer from the table and took a long drink, finishing it off. I'd never felt so much like a fuck up, and I didn't know how I was supposed to make this shit right anymore.

"Well, in the meantime, you better make sure you working overtime to get back on Yara's good side. I guess the good thing is that she didn't give you back yo' ring, so maybe it's some hope for you, bro." He was right. Yara hadn't outright said that the wedding was off, and she hadn't taken the diamond off her finger. That shit made me feel somewhat better about the future. It wasn't like she could just ignore me anyway because we had kids together.

"What you think I should do? Like some romantic shit, 'cause them flowers ain't work," I asked, and his face balled up.

"Nigga, how the fuck I'm s'posed to know! You better get on Pinterest or watch the Hallmark channel!" he grumbled like he wasn't the one who'd given me the flower idea. Then again, I probably shouldn't have been asking him for help since he obviously got that wrong. Whatever I did next needed to blow Yara away, because I wasn't going to stop until I got my family back.

AMARI

"You okay?" I asked Yara as we sat out back behind her house and watched the kids playing. She'd been way more quiet than usual, and although she had her eyes covered with oversized shades, I could tell she wasn't herself.

"Yeah, just tired," she sighed, reclining her lawn chair. Yara was definitely one of the busiest people I knew, so I could understand her being tired. I just didn't think it was all that was going on. After the way Saint had acted the other day, I knew she was going through it with him too, but if she didn't want to tell me about it, I wasn't going to push. Sometimes it was best to keep your man problems to yourself for risk of getting bad advice or feeling torn because of what the next person thought you should do.

I'd gotten plenty of bad advice from Koi's ass when it came to Malik, and it didn't take long before I stopped listening to her when he was brought up. Just because her intimidation tactics worked with some men, it didn't mean it would work for me, and it took me learning that shit the hard way.

"You gotta make sure you're getting your rest, girl. I know it's tough with you and Saint's schedules, but you know I don't got no problem babysitting if you need me to," I told her, meaning every word. SJ and Coco were very good kids, so I wouldn't have a problem keeping an eye on them for her. Yara turned to me and smiled for the first time that day.

"Thank you, I'll definitely keep that in mind."

Little did she know, I was glad to help. She was turning into the friend I didn't know I needed, and I didn't ever mind being there for friends. Well, some friends, because the way Koi was acting and speaking to me was about to have her beat up like a bitch on the street. She'd already made videos about fake friends and talking about me being a doormat to the next bitch. She might not have said any names, but I knew her silly ass was talking about me and Yara. It didn't take a rocket scientist to figure that out, and I knew it was only a matter of time before her thirsty for attention ass did put our names out there. I was starting to see more and more what my mama had been telling me since I'd met Koi. Even back then, my mama saw through her fake ass, but me, it always took me a minute to see people for who they really were. Always trying to see the good in people was a character flaw and I was hoping with age came better discernment.

My phone vibrated on my lap, and I rolled my eyes seeing Malik's name. It had been weeks since he had pulled that disappearing act. He hadn't even called to check on Prince, which was crazy, but just like with other people, I was beginning to see right through him. I never wanted to be the type of woman that kept her kid away from his father, but that was really the direction I was headed in with his ass. My first mind told me to ignore the call, but I still hadn't gotten a chance to talk to him about his one-sided beef with Saint and Psalm. He'd still been online talking shit, and the fact that they weren't acknowledging him only made him fight harder for their attention. It was childish as hell, and I knew soon that shit was going to blow up.

"Hey," I answered dryly just before the voicemail could pick up. I was trying not to get myself worked up and scare him off the phone, so I was hoping he didn't piss me off.

"Where the fuck you at with my son?" he came on fuming,

and I had to pull the phone away from my ear and look at it because he had me fucked up. He'd been the one that was gone and hadn't gave a fuck where our son was, and now he was calling out the blue like he had the right. Everything I'd previously been thinking about playing it cool instantly went out the window. I quickly moved out of earshot of Yara before I exploded.

"Not you callin' me yellin' about where I have Prince when you been in the wind for weeks! You better tone that shit all the way down! You askin' where we at but where the fuck is that daycare money! Where the fuck is you at when I need a babysitter! Shit, where you at when he needs his father in general is the better question!"

"Nothing you just said even matters when you got him around muthafuckas I'm beefing with! Is you dumb!"

"Oh please, nigga, I be on social media too and you ain't beefin' with nobody but yo' self, stupid ass boy!" I smacked my lips. I understood what he meant about keeping Prince safe, but neither Saint nor Psalm were thinking about him so they definitely didn't have a reason to fuck with us. If he was smart then he'd know that.

"No, you're stupid! You got my son all over that nigga Saint's house and anything can happen to him!" That's when I realized that this shit couldn't have anything to do with Prince. For one, nobody even knew about Prince being Malik's son, so the animosity he was sending my way was unwarranted and again stupid.

"Malik, what do you really want? Because you know just like I do that nobody even knows we have a son together." I shook my head with a sigh. The line went quiet for a second and I wondered if he'd hung up, but the minutes were still ticking by when I checked.

"Is you fuckin' that nigga Psalm? On some real shit Amari, I don't want that nigga around my seed, and I ain't playin'. Matter fact, don't even let him know where he lay his head," he demanded, and I cracked up laughing. Him asking about Psalm was only because it'd been made public that we had started following each other. If I was being honest, we'd even been texting and he wasn't as much of an asshole as I'd originally thought, so I'd agreed to go out with him. I figured it wouldn't hurt to be wined and dined for one night, and I was honestly looking forward to it.

"Who I'm fuckin' ain't none of your business! Now who is your business is Prince, so do you want to talk to him? See him?" I knew it was fucked up that I didn't immediately deny fucking with Psalm, and it would probably cause an issue down the line, but the way that nigga spiraled afterward was so satisfying. It was obvious I couldn't get to him through Prince, so I might as well piss him off.

"Bring him to my mama crib," he huffed, and my nose turned up.

"Like right now?"

"Yeah, right now, muthafucka. I'm bouta be over here for a little bit." I don't know why I agreed. Malik really didn't deserve to see Prince when he hadn't made an effort to, and I damn sure didn't want to do it at his mama's house. Marlene wasn't that bad when it came to being in our business, but she was definitely a boy mom who rode for her son. If it wasn't for the fact that she hadn't seen Prince in a while either, then I probably would've insisted that Malik bring his ass to my house instead.

Rolling my eyes at how I'd gotten myself in such a mess, I headed back over to where the kids and Yara were. I wasn't really in a rush to leave, so I didn't schedule my ride for another half hour.

When we finally left and headed to Marlene's house though, Prince was already drowsy, and I realized I probably shouldn't have waited so long. The last thing I wanted was to hear Malik's mouth about him being sleepy or being asleep, so before we got too far I changed my mind and had the driver take me home. I texted Malik instead of calling to let him know, and as expected, his goofy ass left me on read, making me feel like I was right to go home. Before we even made it to our block Prince was knocked out and slobbing.

With his dead weight and my purse, getting up the stairs was a whole struggle, but like always, I managed to get it done. After getting inside, I stripped him out of his clothes and put him to bed in just his boxers and tank top because I didn't want to move him around too much and risk waking him up. My phone buzzed as I headed into my bedroom and I couldn't help smiling when I saw Psalm's name.

"Hey you." I cheesed goofily, lying down across my bed.

"What's up? What you got goin' on?" His deep voice had my insides tingling, and I couldn't remember the last time I felt like that about a nigga. It was crazy that of all people, it was Psalm's ass that had me getting the feels, but between his looks and his flirting, I was on the verge of risking it all.

"Nothing, just got home from Yara's. Prince is taking his nap so I'm probably gonna do the same thing." I shrugged. "What you doin'? In the studio?" I already knew without asking that he was. I'd learned that Psalm was a workaholic and rarely went anywhere besides the studio.

"Ahh, you swear you know some shit," he teased before admitting, "Yeah, I'm in the studio, but I'm probably bouta leave 'cause we finished early."

"Whaaat? The workaholic gone leave early. I'm shocked."

"Yeah, so since I'm leaving, you gone let me spend the rest of the day at the crib with you?" His voice lowered and I shot up in bed. Suddenly, I was all flustered. I hadn't expected him to ask me that. It was cool flirting on the phone and through texts, but in person was a whole different thing. When I took too long to answer, Psalm chuckled lowly. "Damn, you gone leave me hangin' like that?"

"No, I just—"

"It's cool, I already figured out that you're scared of me and shit." I could tell he was teasing, but I still immediately felt the need to prove him wrong. Really, I wasn't scared of him anyway, I was scared of me. It had been so long since I'd had some that I was liable to let him talk me right out my panties.

"Definitely not scared of you," I said smartly and had to squeeze my thighs together when his deep laugh rumbled in my ear.

"Well, what's up then? I'll even bring food. What you hungry for?" That was the quickest way to sway me and he knew it after all our conversations. It only took me a second to decide on some burria though. As soon as we got off the phone I was running around trying to freshen up. After a quick shower, I threw on some sweatpants with a matching cropped sweatshirt and then started working on my hair, which was in a braid out since I didn't need to do a wig video for a few days. It only took a little water and a pick and my curls were looking good and juicy again.

A couple of hours passed before Psalm finally made it, and by then, Prince was up and running around. "Look at you tryna match and shit." He grinned, stepping inside in a pair of gray sweatpants and a white tee, and as usual, he looked good as hell.

"You got all the jokes today, huh?" I watched as he kicked off his Jordan's and tried not to look at his dick.

"I mean, I'm the funniest nigga you know," he joked and tapped my chin playfully.

"Uncle Psalm! Uncle Psalm!" Prince came from around the corner with his little nosy ass. He'd started to call Psalm uncle just like Saint did, and while I kind of thought it was cute, I didn't want him to overstep.

"Prince, I keep telling you Psalm is not your uncle," I sighed, cupping my head in embarrassment, but Psalm instantly shut me down.

"Leave him alone, this my lil' nephew." He nodded, holding out his fist for a pound. "Don't listen to her, lil' Prince, what's good?"

"None." Prince shrugged his little shoulders, trying to sound cool. "Wan see my woom?"

"Yeah, let me check it out." Psalm was already following him to the back where his room was, but I stopped him so I could take the bag of food he was holding. There wasn't a point in me waiting to eat; I'd already seen Prince's room.

By the time they came back, I had our food set out on the coffee table. Psalm had gotten steak tacos and he'd brought me the burria I'd asked for. He didn't end up eating right away though because my baby had talked him into bringing his toy cars back with them. Prince was basically running the show and insisted that we watch *Ninja Turtles* while they played, even though neither paid attention to it the whole time. Our little lunch date had quickly turned into a play date for them, and I couldn't lie. It was cute. My baby never had anybody besides me or my mama to play with until we'd met Yara and Psalm since Malik barely came around. I just hoped that things didn't blow up in my face if Yara ever found out the truth.

Psalm

I had finally gotten Amari to accept a date with my ass, and while I was still trying to tell myself that it was just a scheme, the truth was I was starting to like her. She was smart and about her business, money wise and mama wise, and she was definitely pretty as hell. It didn't take me long to start going out of my way to talk to or be around her ass. It was hard not to. Add the young Prince to the mix and I was stuck. I still didn't like her bitch ass baby daddy, but I was rethinking using her to piss him off. Really, he needed his ass beat for the way he was shitting on his son. He gave Savage Records way more attention than he gave Prince, and that just showed how much of a bitch he really was. I was still considering whether or not I was gone put somebody on him or just do it myself just because. Then again, Amari's softhearted ass would probably feel bad if I did. *Fuck!* When did I start giving a damn about her feelings?

"Where the fuck you goin'?" Saint stood in the doorway as I sprayed on some cologne.

"You nosy as hell, ain't you?" I avoided the question and moved around my room to make sure I had everything. I could still feel him watching as I did and knew he was going to say something, and he proved me right.

"You getting all dressed up for Amari, huh?"

"You up in my business, you need to be getting dressed up for Yara," I told him. He was letting too much time go by without doing something to win his girl back. Since he'd arrived, he had just been moping around my shit, looking like a lost puppy. Even my mama had tried to talk him into standing on business, but the shit he was doing was weak. The mention of Yara had him grumbling like a bitch.

"Yara don't know what she want. I done sent all types of chocolates and roses, but she treat that shit like I picked it up in the alley or something." He looked frustrated, and I almost felt bad for his ass.

"That just means work harder, nigga. Think outside the box or some shit," I advised as I checked out my haircut. It was crispy as expected and so was my beard.

"Ain't that much damn thinking. Her ass just being difficult."

"Whatever, bro, if that's how you feel." I shrugged. I was done arguing with him about what he should do. If he wanted to lose his girl, that was on him. It was already getting close to our reservation time, and I didn't want to be late since I still had to pick up Amari.

I walked right back past his whiny ass and headed out to my truck. I drove all the way to Amari's crib just listening to my playlist on shuffle. By the time I made it I was no longer irritated as she came down the stairs in a little black dress that hugged her curves in all the right places. I met her on the sidewalk and lifted her hand so she could do a spin for me.

"God damn! You clean up good as fuck!" From head to toe she looked like she was about to walk somebody's runway. The compliment had her blushing and a dimpled grin covering her face.

She batted her long eyelashes at me and took in what I was wearing. "You don't look so bad either," she said, and I did a GQ pose. Since we were going to a nice restaurant, I decided on black jeans and a black shirt with some matching Prada sneakers. That was about as dressed up as it was going to get, so I was hoping the restaurant didn't piss me off.

The ride there was like it always was whenever I was around Amari. We talked about all types of shit from work to food, to music or goals, and it was always a vibe. When we got to the restaurant, I wasn't surprised to see it full of people. A weekend at such a nice place was sure to bring out the city. I was glad nobody recognized me, but a couple people came up to Amari before we even got our food.

I watched proudly as she took a picture with somebody and smiled when she caught me still looking. "What?" she tucked her hair behind her ear and asked.

"Nothin', just thinkin' about how you gone be more famous than me."

"I mean, I do a little something, but it's nowhere near you out here making all the bops people listen to, and you're not ugly either. You stepped out here like Metro Boomin' lookin' all good, let the media get wind of you, and you gone have all types of fans and blogs following you around." The side eye she gave me told on her little jealous ass, and I let out a chuckle.

"That's exactly why I ain't tryna be in the spotlight. I save that shit for Saint, he handles it better anyway. Back in the day when we first started, I used to be right by his side, but that shit got old quick for me. I just like to make music and take my ass home," I told her truthfully. It didn't take me long to find out that I didn't like people in my business or feeling like I was in a fishbowl. I wanted to move around freely, and since I wasn't well known, that was easy for me. Amari nodded in understanding and poked out her lips.

"I can see that. It's some things about being on the scene that I don't like, like people feeling entitled to your time and attention, but for the most part the good outweighs the bad...for now." She added that last part quick. She was definitely a different type of person than her friend because Koi loved attention and probably always would. I hadn't even heard her speak that bitch name in a while to be honest. She'd told me that they kind of had a disagreement and she wasn't fucking with her like that, and I was happy about that shit. I couldn't stand that damn girl.

They finally brought our food out and I laughed at how excited she got. Amari was a true foodie and was greedy as hell, but I liked that shit. She never tried to act like she didn't eat or tried to pick at food like some other bitches I'd talked to before, including my baby mama.

Things were going good, and I was actually enjoying myself until I saw Malice's goofy ass come stomping through the restaurant. He looked crazy in the wife beater and basketball shorts he was wearing, and I was confused as fuck on how he even got in. When I saw the maître d running up behind him, I realized his weird ass had probably forced his way in, considering that he was with two other niggas.

"Look at this shit here! Not my baby mama out here being a hoe with Psalm Savage goofy ass!" He stopped a few feet from our table, talking loud and disturbing the other guests, and that's when I saw his ass was recording. I'd been trying to spare him, to be honest. We both knew I'd beat his ass, but he'd already played with me too many times.

"Malik, what the hell are you doin'?" Amari sucked her teeth and tried to shield her face from his camera.

"Bro, take yo' lame ass on before I beat yo' ass like yo' daddy didn't," I warned lowly, hoping he'd take the hint and leave, but he was too pumped up to listen to reason.

"Nigga, fuck you! I'm not one of those little bitch ass niggas on yo' label! You can't tell me shit!"

"Please don't pay him any attention." She tried to stop me as I stood, but it was too late.

"Look, I know times is hard, and if you're really hungry, I'll let you get the rest of the bread off the table as long as you and your little minions leave." One thing that nigga hated was for somebody to make it seem like he was broke. Multiple times on his lives he was being called out for not really having money, and that had to be true because he spent more time online than he did in the actual studio. He was still trying to promote his first diss since nobody had signed his ass yet. That independent life only worked if you were actually good, and Malice was mediocre at best.

"Suck my d—" I didn't let him finish before I hit his ass in the mouth and blood instantly started gushing out. The two niggas with him looked like they were about to run up and snake me, but they both backed up when I set my eyes on them. They snatched their homeboy up from the floor and dragged his unconscious ass out as the other restaurant guests clapped. Everybody was happy for his ass to go after causing such a disruption. The only issue was that he was probably online as usual when he came in, so now whoever was on that live had seen me with Amari and had also seen him get his ass knocked out.

"Oh my gosh, that was so embarrassing! Now you know that Malice is my baby daddy." She shielded her eyes from the other guests like they wouldn't be able to see her. "I'm really sorry about that. He usually doesn't give a damn what I have going on, but I guess now since you're here it pushed him over the edge."

"It's cool," I dismissed, picking my fork back up. "So that's Young Prince's daddy, huh?"

"Yes, unfortunately." She was finally focusing back on her food.

"No wonder he gets his real nigga gene from you. It definitely ain't from that nigga." We shared a laugh and, not too long after, finished our food. I was glad that despite her bitch ass baby daddy showing up, it hadn't killed the mood.

When I walked her up onto her porch after our date was over, I was expecting a kiss and a goodnight, but Amari pulled me into the hallway behind her. I was only confused for all of a few seconds because once we reached her apartment, she was working her way out of her dress and trying hard to get my pants undone. The wine had flowed freely so we were both a little tipsy, but that didn't affect my carrying her to her bedroom as our tongues danced.

I dropped her on the bed and eyed her body in the black underwear she wore, and my dick grew even harder. "You sure you tryna do this?" I asked as she sat up on the side of the bed and released my dick, smiling when it sprang free.

"Positive," she moaned, swallowing me whole. As she slurped and sucked the life out of me, she looked into my eyes, allowing her saliva to run down the sides of her face.

"Shiiiit, suck this muthafucka then," I hissed, grabbing the back of her head and guiding her. The entire time, she hummed, making a vibration within her throat, and my toes curled. I was already on the verge of shooting down her throat, but I wanted to feel her. "Come here." She released me with a wet popping sound and instantly went in for a kiss. We helped each other undress completely, only stopping long enough for me to slip on a condom before I climbed on top of her. My dick was already tapping at her center, and she moaned into my mouth as I teased her, barely slipping the tip in before pulling away.

"Psalm," she whined, wrapping her legs around my waist to keep me from moving.

"What you want, baby?" I kissed her neck as she writhed beneath me. I wanted her to say what she wanted me to do to her, and was trying to wait until she did, but my dick felt like it was about to break it was so hard.

"Please...I want you so bad." She damn near sounded like she was about to cry.

"What you want me to do?" I continued teasing, and her eyes shot open, full of fire.

"I want you to fuck me, Psalm!" That was all I needed to hear. I wasted no time sliding into her silky walls and immediately had to stop for a second.

"Fuck, baby, you feel so fuckin' good." I hadn't even did shit but enter her and I was already on the verge of busting through the condom. Amari had the softest, tightest pussy I'd ever felt. I covered her lips with mine, kissing her to try and take my mind off coming, before finally beginning to rock on top of her.

I cuffed her legs in the crooks of my arms so I could watch my dick gliding into her and marveled at the way her cream covered the entire length.

"Oooh, *Psalm*, right there!" she screamed and rolled her hips to match my strokes. I kept drilling right where she told me to until I felt her walls clenching and contracting around me, letting me know she was coming. Using her legs, I turned her over and entered her from behind. I laid on top of her so that my chest was flush against her back as I stroked her slowly and sucked her neck.

"This my pussy now, Amari. Only mine!" I growled in her ear before sticking my tongue inside of it.

"Only yoooourrsss," she repeated as I slammed into her now, dick growing harder with each pump.

"Fuck, I'm bouta nut!" I bit into her shoulder as I released into the condom for what seemed like forever. Amari whimpered beneath me and caressed my head while I tried to get my breathing back to normal. When I finally rolled off of her, I frowned seeing that the condom wasn't there anymore. "Fuck!"

SAINT

Everybody had been telling me I needed to try harder when it came to the shit with me and Yara, but I didn't know what that looked like. I'd throw money at the problem by sending her gifts and shit, but none of that seemed to be working because she was still giving me the same dry ass energy. Even when it came to the kids and shit, she didn't have much to say to me when I went to pick them up or went over to just spend time with them. It seemed like everything my brother had been warning me about was coming true. Yara wasn't fucking with me and I was missing the shit I'd taken for granted, but it was going to be over my dead body if I saw her with another nigga. It sounded crazy, but I felt like I deserved the chance to make shit right before she truly moved on, and since she was still wearing my ring, I still had a chance.

Today, I was going to do something different, and I just hoped she acted right. Since I still knew her recording schedule, I knew when I pulled up at our house that she was home and she wasn't busy, but I had my OG come before me so that we could have a sitter. With that much thought, there was no way she was going to say no, or at least I was praying she wouldn't. In an effort to respect her space, I hadn't been using my key whenever I dropped by, so when I came on the porch, I hit the bell like I was a damn guest at my own shit for real. A second later, my mama came to the door and gave me an encouraging smile.

"Hey baby, she's in the kitchen washing one of those damn wigs," she complained, rolling her eyes, but pulled me back when I started toward the kitchen. "Now I'm helping you Saint, but I need you to know that it better not be a next time! If that girl comes to me crying behind yo' ass again, you ain't gone like the monster I turn her into." I couldn't even do shit but shake my head at that shit, but I was glad that she considered Yara like a daughter in real life and wanted to protect her, even from me. Instead of arguing with her about that shit, I just nodded, and the warning look she had on her face disappeared and was replaced with a smile. "Okay, good luck." She blew me a kiss before going back toward the kitchen. *Crazy ass!*

"Ohhh, look who decided to grace us with his presence! Hey, son!" she sang as we stepped into the room where Yara was at the sink. She looked at the both of us like we were crazy as hell, and I knew that was mostly my mama's fault for using a fake British accent. Everybody already knew that she couldn't act for shit, and that was because whenever she was supposed to pretend to not know some shit, she used that voice. Yara twisted her lips as she rolled her eyes over to me, ignoring my mama's dramatics.

"Hey, Saint." Her voice was robotic as hell as she pointed toward the kids' playroom. "The kids are in there." When she realized I wasn't taking my ass up to where they were, she tilted her head at me, and my mama kicked me in the fucking shin. I shot her evil little ass a look before turning my attention back to Yara.

"I was actually trying to see if you wanted to take a ride with me...like old times?" I could see that she hadn't been expecting that, and I gave myself a pat on the back for confusing her.

"If you wanna go, I'll stay with the kids," my mama offered, and I made a mental note to get her something nice for being a good wingman.

"A ride where? 'Cause I need to be back in time to get dinner ready." Yara stopped working her hands in the sink long enough to ask.

"Nigga, around the city," I said, and we both laughed. "You know what it is." I hoped that her laughter meant she was leaning toward letting me take her, and it did because she quickly rang out the wig and set it aside.

"Okay, I'll go, but I'm not staying out long, Saint," she warned, pointing a finger at me.

"You got it." A goofy ass grin spread across my face as she came around and headed to the front for her shoes.

"You ain't slick either, Angel!" Yara called out over her shoulder, and my mama just shrugged because her crazy ass didn't care either way. Once Yara came back, we headed out in my Hellcat with the music blasting. I looked between Yara and the road, realizing that she looked good as fuck with the sun shining in on her. Besides her lashes, her face was makeup free and her natural hair was in two French braids. I'd obviously picked the perfect day for the ride because she even looked like how she did back in the day. Real shit, it was hard to keep my eyes off her, and I wondered how the hell Koi had managed to steal my attention when I had Yara's gorgeous ass all this time. "What you staring at?" she finally asked after she'd caught me for the tenth time, and I was glad that there was a smile on her face instead of the mug I'd been receiving lately.

"Shiiit, you," I admitted shamelessly. "You're beautiful as fuck, Ya."

"Thank you." She blushed, trying hard to stop another smile from coming through as she turned to the window. We were riding down Lakeshore Drive, and I was even playing old ass Pleasure P just like I did when we first met.

"Remember we used to ditch school up here?" I smirked as all our teenage memories popped up, and Yara giggled.

"Yeah, and our ass got caught that one time 'cause you still had on yo' uniform! That police officer was ready to lock both of us up after the way you talked about his toupee!" By now, she was cracking up with tears coming out of her eyes, and I swear the sound of her laugh was like music to my ears.

"Man, first of all, that nigga knew he coulda let us go! He wanted to try and talk shit, so I had to go on that hair hat he was wearing!" I shrugged. That nigga was talking too much that day so he had to get it.

"Oh my gosh! You asked him if he put his wife coochie hair up there!"

"I mean, in my defense, it did look like some damn pube hair." I could still remember exactly how that shit looked and would probably be able to identify his ass if I ever saw him again.

"You were crazy," Yara said, shaking her head once she'd finally calmed down.

"Shit, I remember you throwing some shit in there once he started talking 'bout my shoes." I eyed her, and she blinked coyly.

"Well, he shouldn't have been talking 'bout my man," she huffed. "I had to have yo' back." Her voice was soft and a silence fell over the car as I reached over and gripped her hand up in mine. The fact that she didn't immediately pull away had me feeling like a lame for being so excited from something so simple. It felt good to just be at peace for the moment, and I just hoped the shit lasted.

After I dropped Yara back off, I headed over to Koi's crib. She'd been calling me from all types of different numbers and making threats online that I knew were directed at me. I had been doing good at ignoring her for the most part, but I didn't like feeling like a looming threat was coming my way. I was barely back in Yara's good graces, and I wasn't about to let Koi's silly ass fuck that up.

When I pulled up on her, she was just getting home, and as soon as she saw me, she smirked sneakily. She probably thought she'd beat me down to give in to her shit, but her pussy was the last thing on my mind. Shit, after losing Yara, everything about

Koi was a bad omen, and I wasn't going down that road with her ass ever again.

She waited while I climbed out and then immediately tried to run over to hug me, but I stiff armed her quick, making her sputter. I didn't even want her to touch me. She squinted, trying to read me, but I was blank as fuck as I grabbed her arm. "Let's go talk inside," I said, letting her go once she started walking toward her apartment. When we got inside, she tried again, and I held her off me again.

"Oh my god, are we back on this shit again? What's your problem?" she asked, crossing her arms petulantly.

"You are. I told you already I'm done fucking with you, so stop fuckin' callin' me and stop making them lame ass posts about me and my girl. I'm only gone tell you this shit one time before I lay yo' goofy ass out." My tone was calm, but the look in my eyes should've let her know I wasn't playing.

"So now y'all all in love, but you was just fucking me in the bathroom! You're the only muthafucka that give a damn about that bitch—" Her words were cut short as I reached out and grabbed her throat, applying enough pressure so that it was impossible to breath.

"Leave. Us. Alone! You hear me! Don't contact me. Don't make no posts or story times or whatever the fuck you been doin'! It's not getting my attention in the way you think, and if you keep playing with me, I'ma kill yo' stupid ass!" I growled close to her ear before shoving her away. Being dramatic, she fell into a chair, coughing and trying to suck in air. I felt like we had an understanding until I was walking out the door and she tried to call me back with tear-filled eyes.

"Saint! Saint, please! Don't do this!" She was struggling to catch her breath and she was still trying to beg. "Is this 'cause of Amari? Did that bitch say something to make you act like this! You literally ain't been right since she came around!" I really didn't know why she was trying to blame Amari for what I was doing, but it was all me. I still didn't even know how I felt about her, but after her being around for a while and Psalm getting to know her, it was obvious she wasn't going anywhere for a while.

"Yo, I don't know what you talkin' about. Amari ain't said shit to me, but what I'm saying to you is to let this shit go. Find another nigga and leave me the fuck alone!" I shook her off since she'd come over and grabbed my arm to stop me from leaving. This was going to be my last time trying to get my point across, because if she didn't stay away like I'd told her ass, she was going to meet her maker.

This time she smartly stayed back when I went to leave, watching me evilly while rubbing her throat. Something told me I would have to be careful moving forward with her ass, and I planned to. I'd had a good time with my baby mama, and I was hoping shit would continue to go well with us until I was able to get my damn family back. Koi just needed to stay the fuck away from me indefinitely.

Koi

The way Saint left had me feeling some type of way, but I wasn't crazy enough to run up behind a nigga that had damn near just choked me out. He obviously needed some time to get his mind right and I was going to allow that, but he was highly mistaken if he thought I was about to let go so easily. As far as I was concerned, Saint was mine and would stay mine. Shit, I was so thirsty at this point that I was willing to share with Yara, which was some shit I was not used to doing. I stood in the same spot for a few minutes, just staring at the door before finally going to my room so I could check my neck in the mirror. Thankfully there wasn't anything visible there. The last thing I needed was for people to see a nigga's handprint on my neck. Then again, if people saw it, I could blame Saint and get his stupid ass locked up! That would serve him right for putting his hands on me in the first place. Some time in jail would always have a nigga thinking about his actions, but if I got him locked up, I probably wouldn't be able to come back from that.

After checking my neck from multiple angles, I grabbed my keys and headed over to Amari's house. We hadn't talked since our little spat at the influencer event, but if anybody knew the inside scoop on Saint and Yara, it was her new best friend. She'd been hanging out with Amari so much that the bitch Jasmin wasn't even around like that anymore, which made so much sense because Amari and Yara probably got along so well because they were both shitty friends.

My phone rang on the passenger seat, and I rolled my eyes, seeing my agent's number, but I still answered anyway because she may have had a job for me. I might have been a lot of things, but I wasn't a fool when it came to my coins.

"What's up, Jess?" I put on my chipper white girl voice.

"*Koi*, I have a hosting event for you. It's this weekend at..." She went silent, and I could hear her papers fluttering in the background as she tried to find the information. I hated when she did that because it would have made more sense to have all that shit ready when she called me, but she was obviously ditzy. If she wasn't the reason I stayed so booked, I would've fired her a long time ago. "Oh, it's at Club X with Amari, the girl that does beauty and hair. You know she's become a little of an internet sensation since it was revealed that she was that rapper's baby mama." She sounded excited, but my nose instantly turned up. Amari had been popping up everywhere, and it was starting to get on my nerves. The fact that she was getting clout off of Malice's video was tacky. How did anybody think it was cool that she was out with another nigga and got her baby daddy knocked out? Having to share a club with her for money wasn't my idea of a good time, but I could probably make it work to my benefit in the long run.

"How much?" I asked flippantly, interrupting her droning.

"It will be fifteen thousand—"

"To split?" I cut her off, ready to curse her ass out if she said it was only a few thousand-dollar bag.

"Oh no, you'll get the whole fifteen," she rushed to say, and I calmed down a little. Fifteen was on the low end of what I could make at the club, but I'd take it just because it was easy work, plus I got to drink and just look pretty.

"How much is she gettin'?"

"Ohhhh, she's getting twenty," she said that shit like it was cool and my attitude instantly returned.

"How is she getting more than me when she just came on the scene, Jess?" There was no way that bitch thought that made sense, and as she babbled, I realized that she did.

"Well, she is associated with Savage Records, so that puts her in high demand, and if she brings Psalm or hell, even Saint and his fiancée, she'd probably get more. You know people love a good—"

"A good scandal, a good romance, and good drama," I finished her sentence and grit my damn teeth. I had to stop myself from telling her that I had all three and had been in the Savage Records circle for longer than Amari's ass, but Jess would definitely want to use that nugget of information, and I knew Saint wasn't going to be happy about that.

"Exactly, so let me iron out a few details, and then I'll send the information over to you," she said, hanging up just as I pulled in front of Amari's apartment. *There is no way that girl is getting that much money and still living in this shitty apartment*, I thought, turning my nose up. I guess it wasn't so bad. It wasn't like she had roaches like some people, and it was a pretty clean building. It was just small as hell.

I made it up to her apartment and knocked, cursing myself for not calling to make sure she was even there. I was so used to being able to just pop up on her when she didn't have shit going on that I hadn't thought about it. Thankfully, a second later, I heard the locks turning, and Amari opened it with a mug on her face like she had the right to be mad at me.

"Hey, girl! I came to offer you a truce." I gave her a phony smile and pressed my hands together like I was begging. She just stared at me for a second before finally moving out of the way to let me in. My eyes scanned the room and I realized nothing had changed about the apartment. She hadn't bought anything new like a bigger TV or new furniture. She was crazy as hell to have a nigga with as much money as Psalm and wasn't using it every chance she got. It seemed like I hadn't taught her shit in all the years we'd been friends. When I got with Saint I had him buying all types of shit, but that's why we were different. She'd probably never ask a nigga for nothing, even when they had no problem asking for pussy.

"What you wanted to talk about, Koi? I have something to do in a while, soooo."

Ooooh, not her dismissing me, I thought with a raised brow. Amari was trying to get a little backbone. I turned around, doing a good job of showing my irritation with her on my face.

"Well, I was wondering if you were going to do the Club X appearance with me this weekend?"

"Wait, that's with you?" Her forehead wrinkled, and I nodded.

"Yeah, they reached out to you already, right? I had my agent add you on with me so you can make some extra money since you claim I never help you with shit like that," I said sarcastically. She had really tried to act like I wasn't shit for not wanting to put her on. My brand was important, and there was no guarantee that she would have popped with those kitchen do's and shit.

"Oh, um, thanks." Her eyes shifted uncomfortably and I plopped down on her couch.

"You're welcome. So what's been new since we haven't talked?" I tried to sound nonchalant, but she still seemed weird, like she wasn't sure if I was really cool, which was crazy because we'd been friends for years. Hell, she knew me better than that Yara bitch.

"Koi, I appreciate you getting me the job and all, but now that I know you're involved, I'll probably cancel. We're not gonna act like you wasn't just at that day party talking to me out the side of your neck, and you didn't even apologize. Really, I think you should leave 'cause I'm not tryna have no problems, but I also don't want you in my crib." She read me so fast that I was still searching for the words as she opened the door to let me out. Flabbergasted, I looked around like I'd find what I wanted to say just lying around before I finally got up.

"Amari, girl—"

"I don't even need the apology because you've never really been a good friend and I always overlooked it, but I'm not accepting that shit no more." My neck snapped back like I'd been slapped, and in a way, I had with the tongue lashing she'd just given me. Without anything to say, I flipped my hair and exited her little raggedy ass apartment. She had me just as fucked up as Saint did, but what she was going to find out was that I was the most disrespectful bitch I knew, and if she wanted to go low, I'd go to the devil's headquarters. I'd barely gotten across the threshold when she slammed the door shut, only pissing me off even more.

Pulling up my contacts, I called a number I'd only used on occasion when I wanted some money or some dick and Saint wasn't around. He picked up right away like I knew he would.

"What you want, Koi?"

"Oooh, why you and yo' bald head ass baby mama so damn mean today? Is it 'cause yo' lip still swollen?" I poked and almost laughed at how I could hear Malik's breathing increasing on the line. I'd been messing around with Malik for almost as long as Prince was alive and it always went under Amari's nose. She thought I couldn't stand him and to an extent, I couldn't. We mostly had hate sex, but he would still run those pockets when asked and that was why the night she was looking for him for daycare money, he was ducking her because he'd given it to me. He'd sent me the CashApp while I sat in her room waiting on her to finish her video, but I'd never tell her that. I never wanted shit between me and Malik to get exposed. For one, Saint probably wouldn't forgive me, and I couldn't have that.

"Fuck you and that bitch!" He was still very much mad, or maybe it was because his baby mama was such a sore spot for him. Either way, none of that was my business.

"Well, that's what I'm calling you for. I had a bad day and I'm in need of something a little rough. Can you still eat pussy with a swollen lip?"

"Can you eat dick with a swollen lip? 'Cause if you keep talkin', yo' shit gone be matching mine," he threatened, and I rolled my eyes because he'd never put his hands on me or else he'd be going straight to jail. I didn't play that domestic violence shit when I used my face and body to make money.

"I'm on my way," I said, hanging up on him. If I let him, he'd talk my ear off trying to get information about Amari, and I didn't have any more than he did, considering that we were no longer friends according to her. It was okay with me though, fuck that bitch.

Yara

I walked through the grocery store, regretting actually taking my ass outside instead having some groceries delivered. For one, I had Coco up front and Saint's little bad ass in the buggy part, which was taking up a lot of space. Then they were both loud as hell, and I realized that I should've left them with Saint. Every person I passed was looking at me extra hard. Probably wondering why I hadn't left them at home too. I really was over the trip in general, but I was too far to turn back now. I walked from aisle to aisle, putting things in the cart that we needed for sure and telling SJ no when he asked for something I wasn't getting. I had already worked it out that I wasn't going to be there long when Coco started throwing her pacifier. I was able to catch it the first couple of times, but then it bounced off of me and hit the floor. That unlocked a new level of excitement for her so she began aiming for the floor.

"Girl, next time, I'm not getting it back for you," I huffed, making her fall into a fit of laughter. "You're laughing, but I promise you will be without a pacifier, boo."

"Damn, do you always go around denying babies of their pacifiers?" a deep voice rumbled from behind me, and I turned around to see a nigga was that was so fine I had to clutch the cart.

He was tall and caramel-skinned with a bald fade. He was checking off all the boxes and I could tell he had money just from the watch he was wearing.

"Damn, do you always go around eavesdropping on other people's conversations?" I tilted my head up at him with a smirk, and God, when that man smiled back at me, I really grew weak in the knees.

"Touché." He nodded. "So can I have the name of the woman that put me in my place?" he tried to throw it in there, and before I could decline and flash my ring like I'd done so many times before, I remembered I wasn't wearing it and said fuck it. Saint was out here talking to whoever he wanted and acting single, and right now, I was actually single.

"Yara, and you are?"

"Oooh, that's different, and it matches mine a lil' bit," he said, and I was expecting for his name to really be similar to mine. "I'm Isiah." He smiled, and I cracked up laughing.

"Sir, our names are nowhere near each other!"

"Damn, you don't think so?" he joked. I hadn't talked to him for even five minutes, but I could tell I liked his personality. At least, I liked what he had shown so far.

"No, I don't, but I'll see you around, Isiah." My tone was flirty as I went to walk away, but he stopped me.

"Look, I usually don't do this, but I just feel like I can't let you go without trying my luck. I'll make it easy for you and just give you my number. That way, if you wanna get up with me, you can, and if not, you can just throw it away. Deal?"

I liked that he hadn't immediately started giving it to me and had waited until I agreed to the deal. It was different than what I was used to and intriguing. "Okay, deal." I smirked, preparing to save him in my phone, but he handed me a business card. "Okay, well, we'll see what fate says, Isiah Thomas." I read his name off the card and was impressed at his title as a lawyer. He lamely crossed his fingers with a smile as I walked off, feeling all giddy.

For some reason, after that, shopping wasn't so bad and I

finished a short time later. Saint waited until we got in the car to start questioning me though.

"Ma, what was his name?" I froze, unsure of how to answer, as I strapped Coco in her car seat. I didn't want to seem like I was trying to be sneaky, but I also wasn't trying to give him too much information. Saint was the type of kid who dropped pieces of stories whenever he told them. So he may half snitch today by randomly bringing the man's name up, then the next day he'd drop that I took some paper from him. Kids were weird like that. I thought carefully about what I was going to say before just telling him.

"Oh, his name is Isiah." Thinking that would be all, I put my attention back on strapping in the baby, but as soon as I was behind the wheel, he was back at it.

"Is Zaya yo' friend?"

Shit! He was definitely interested in who that man was, and suddenly, I was feeling like a teenager whose younger sibling had caught them doing something wrong. "Uhhh, no baby, he was just somebody being nice." I shifted my eyes with the lie and was already trying to think of a way to get rid of that damn card, which was crazy because I wasn't with anyone at the moment. If anything, I should've felt justified talking to another man, but here I was lying.

Saint had been trying hard to win me back and I'd been receptive to it so far. The gifts weren't really winning it for me, but the time and the thought he was putting in was slowly making me open up. Like the day we took the drive and reminisced. That had been sweet and different, and so had the little family date nights he'd been planning, but that didn't mean I wasn't still mad as hell. Saint needed to restore my trust in him and I really didn't know how he could do that. Even with him coming over I still felt like he was leaving to go lay up with some bitch. Then I still didn't know who it was and that bothered the fuck out of me. Did she look better? Was she thicker than me? Every time I thought I was moving past the betrayal, shit like that let me know I hadn't.

As if I'd willed him up, my phone rang with a FaceTime call from Saint and instead of answering, I just stared at it until it stopped. I'd pissed myself off that quick and now I didn't even want to hear his voice. My feelings had been all over the place. One minute, I was ready to forgive him because I missed him, and then the next, I wanted to burn our house down with him in it. I waited a second to see if he'd call back and was thankful when he didn't, but then I immediately wondered if that was because he'd gotten distracted by his bitch. Before I could stop myself, I was reaching for my phone to call his ass.

"What's up, bae? You busy?" he answered quickly, but my eyes still narrowed in suspicion.

"Don't call me bae!" I went off, not caring how crazy I sounded. "Why didn't you call me right back when I didn't answer, nigga?" My voice was full of accusation as I sat with the car running. The line went silent and I was surprised when Saint chuckled in my ear.

"Yo, you for real right now?" He sounded like he thought I was crazy, and that just irritated me more.

"Would I have asked if I wasn't?" This time the silence that followed my nastiness didn't end with a laugh. Instead, I heard him shuffling around and his background grew quieter.

"I didn't call back because I assumed you were busy, that's why I asked, Yara. Why you tweaking, bro? What's up with you? We been cool and now you trippin' out of nowhere."

"Well, when a nigga che—" I stopped myself as I looked in the rearview at my babies who were staring straight in my mouth. They didn't know or understand what was going on. I'd tried not to badmouth their father or argue in front of them since Saint had left home, and here I was low key doing both.

"Naw, gone head and say that shit."

"I'm actually on my way home with the kids, so I'll just talk to you when I get home," I pivoted, rolling my eyes as I finally put the car in gear to pull off.

"Ayite bet, I'ma meet you there," Saint said, hanging up

before I could decline. I cursed under my breath. I wasn't in the mood to argue with him, and that was exactly what was going to happen once he showed up at the house.

"Was that my daddy?" SJ asked from the back seat, and I clenched my teeth.

"Yes baby, he's about to meet us at the house." He instantly began cheering, which had Coco laughing and clapping. As mad as I was, I couldn't deny that our babies loved his dirty draws.

"Is he staying?" That was the thing I was dreading. I wasn't ready for Saint to come home yet and probably never would be, but I didn't want my baby worried about that. Instead, I hit him with a 'we'll see,' and thankfully he seemed satisfied with that for now.

When we made it home a short time later, Saint was already there, and once again, SJ cheered, seeing his car in the driveway. I let him out first so he could go find his daddy, while I unstrapped Coco and popped the trunk. I carried my baby toward the house, and as soon as she saw her daddy walking to us with SJ in his arms, she started showing out. He reached for her with his free arm, so I handed her over and headed back to the car to get the bags.

"Man, what the fuck you doin'? You know you don't carry shit when I'm here," he chastised once he saw the bags I'd managed to grab out. If I was being honest, I was glad he'd stopped me because I knew damn well I didn't want to do that shit, but I would've just to try and prove a point. Shrugging, I dropped them with an attitude and reached to at least take Coco, but her little traitor ass only hugged him tighter like she didn't even know me. "I said I got it."

I threw my hands up and stormed into the house, leaving him and the kids. Since he was going to handle everything, I headed to our room for a shower. Just the short amount of time I'd been standing out there had me sweating bullets and I was so ready for snow. I set the water on lukewarm in hopes that it would keep me from overheating. It honestly felt so good that I didn't want to get out, even after knowing I'd been in for a long ass time. After I finished cleaning my body, I wrapped one of my huge, plush towels around myself and instantly got annoyed seeing Saint waiting for me on our bed. Barely giving him a second glance, I went over to my dresser to grab my favorite body lotion and some clothes to throw on. He stayed silent until he saw me about to go back into the bathroom and quickly jumped in my way.

"Now you just doin' the most,, bruh. What the fuck is yo' problem?" he pressed, forcing me backward.

"I don't have a problem." I was nonchalant, shrugging as I tried to move past him again.

"Oh, you don't?" He blocked me and leaned down into my face.

"Nope." My lips popped on the word, making me smile inwardly at how angry he was getting. It definitely served him right considering how pissed off he had me since our break.

Saint laughed in a way that let me know he didn't find shit funny and once again started backing me away from the bathroom as he spoke. "I know what's wrong with yo' crazy ass. I ain't made that pussy cum in a while." He nodded like he was finally understanding, and I sucked my teeth. Of course, he'd reduce my issues with him to me needing an orgasm.

"Boy, fuck you!"

"That's what I'm tryna do. You're the one playin'." He smirked as my legs hit the bed, stopping me from running any further. Tugging at my towel, his eyes gleamed in amusement when I struggled to keep it around me and still hold on to the things in my arms.

"Nigga—"

"Oooh, what do we have here?" He caught me off guard and slipped his hands between my thighs, way too happy to find moisture there. I felt like a weak ass bitch to be honest. The last thing I should've been was turned on, but between his masculine scent and his fine ass pressing me, my body wasn't connecting with my brain. I shuddered as he swiped his finger between my lips and then brought it to his mouth with a low moan. "Mmmhmm, you bouta let me in that pussy, Ya?"

"No." Even as I said it, my pussy clenched and Saint raised a skeptical brow.

"No? That doesn't sound very convincing, baby," he spoke, taking one last step that landed me on the bed. Before I could get back up, he'd dropped to his knees and had my legs over his shoulders. That first swipe of his tongue had my back arching, and I was too paralyzed to get up.

"Saiiiiint!" Holding my thighs apart firmly, he latched on to my clit and all of the fight left my body. I raised my hips to feed him more of my pussy and he let out a taunting moan.

"Mmhmm."

He slithered his tongue up and down my slit, stopping every time he reached my nub to suck it into his mouth. My orgasm was already creeping up and I clawed at the sheets as I grinded against his face. "Baby!" I whimpered, tossing my head back. I came long and hard, body still twitching once Saint stood to his feet, but I quickly got myself together when I saw his pants drop. Suddenly, I was disgusted that I'd allowed him to touch me. I wondered if he'd put his mouth on that bitch or if he'd made her cum so hard she was cross-eyed. It wasn't the first time I'd had those thoughts, but somehow having them after an orgasm had me tight, and I was mad that I couldn't even bask in the glow. The shit-eating grin on his face made it worse, and I put my foot in his chest before he could come closer. That sent him back a couple of feet, and I used the opportunity to get my ass up. Any other time the stupid look on his face as he stood there with a hard dick probably would've had me laughing, but there wasn't shit funny happening at the moment.

"Where the fuck you goin'?" Saint asked stupidly, wiping my juices from his face.

"I'm going to shower again. Thanks for the head though." His mouth dropped in disbelief as I darted around him for the bathroom. He tried unsuccessfully to grab me, and I dipped just out of reach. I'd barely made it inside and locked the door before he was banging on it.

"Stop playin' bro, I know you ain't bouta leave my dick this hard!"

"And is!" I laughed, walking away to turn the shower on. I continued ignoring him, and eventually, he got fed up enough to leave me alone, but I knew he wasn't going to let that shit slide.

Amari

I sat in VIP with Yara and Jazmin actively ignoring Koi's desperate ass. After finding out about her being involved in the club appearance, I started to decline it but realized it would be stupid to turn down some money on her account. Instead, I decided to hit her where it hurt by inviting Yara. I even made it a stipulation that we had separate VIPs, and I was surprised when they obliged me. Now she was sitting across from us shooting daggers my way, but I wasn't going to give her the satisfaction of paying her any attention.

"Okkkaaaaaay! Fuck it up!"

"That's that fuck a nigga twerk right there!" Me and Jazmin egged Yara on while she shook her ass to the beat. I was being a little messy because I knew Koi was watching, but truthfully, I was happy for Yara. After the shit with Saint, I knew she'd been going through it, so to see her carefree was refreshing. A small part of me felt like I should use the opportunity to let her know what I knew, but at the same time, I didn't want to involve myself. I knew firsthand how some women were when it came to their niggas. She may know that he was fucking somebody on the side, but if I was the one bringing any information to her, she may very well turn her misguided anger onto me. The optics of it all just wasn't a good look, and I wasn't trying to take that chance, especially if she ended up getting back with Saint. That shit would be awkward as hell.

"Ain't that your girl over there?" Yara asked, pointing across the way as we all sat down. I already knew she was talking about Koi's ass, but I looked anyway, and just like I thought, she still had her nose turned up.

"Yeah, that's her." I lifted my drink to my lips, hoping she'd move on, but that wasn't happening.

"Why she lookin' like that?" Jazmin chimed in, not even trying to hide her disdain.

"Like what?"

"Like she want me to punch her funny lookin' ass in the mouth… No offense, Amari, but I don't like that phony bitch."

Normally, I would've felt some type of way and defended Koi, but she'd burned her last bridge with me. "Do what you feel." I shrugged nonchalantly and both of their eyes stretched wide. The last thing I was trying to do was talk about my issues with Koi, but from the way they were looking at me, I knew that's exactly what they were expecting.

"I thought y'all was cool. That's the only reason I didn't clock her for that funny shit at the party," Yara grumbled, and I swallowed hard. Koi's shade at the party had been obvious but Yara hadn't mentioned it, so I didn't think she'd even remembered. Saint's funky ass attitude after the fact probably played a big role in that, but now that she was bringing it up, my heart dropped a little.

"What funny shit? I'll slap that bitch right now!" Jazmin was already moving to get up, but Yara pulled her back.

"Girl, ain't nobody thinking about her ass. You know how she is, she's always throwing rocks and hiding her damn hands," Yara scoffed, describing Koi's messy ass perfectly. "I ain't even have time to think about her though, because Saint started with his bullshit."

"Speak of the god damn devil," Jazmin said, eyes shifting to the entrance. "Don't look now, but here he comes."

Surprise then irritation clouded Yara's face as she followed Jazmin's gaze down to the first floor where Saint and Psalm had the crowd parting like the Red Sea. Despite being annoyed that he'd brought his brother, butterflies still filled my belly at the sight of my man. As usual, his face was set in a permanent mug, which grew even deeper when the DJ announced their arrival. The club went up as expected and multiple cameras flashed as they made their way to our section.

"Ugh! Did you know his ass was coming?" Yara huffed, breaking me out of my thoughts.

"Hell no! Psalm said he might come through but he didn't say shit about bringing Saint with him," I quickly cleared up. I didn't even like Saint so I definitely wouldn't have set her up for him.

"We can leave if you want," Jazmin wasted no time saying, but Yara waved her off with an eye roll.

"Naw, if I try to leave his ass ain't gone do shit but cause a scene or follow me anyway." She went to pour herself another drink just as the men reached us. Saint sat down next to Yara, making her suck her teeth, while Psalm stopped in front of me smelling like heaven. He smirked as he leaned forward to give me a kiss, and for a second, I got lost in his soft ass lips before I remembered his brother's presence and bit him.

"Why you bring him? I told you not to tell him Yara was gone be here."

"Shiiiit, he already knew she was with you 'cause my OG's big mouth ass got the kids." He shrugged coolly, licking his lips. "Do that shit again though." Even though I knew he was teasing, my pussy still thumped just from that simple act, and I obliged, this time nibbling on his lip a little longer.

"You better chill before we have to cut this shit short." His warning was followed up with a lustful stare that had me ready to do just that. It was crazy that in such a short amount of time, I'd gone from hating Psalm to wanting to be in his space all day every day. We'd literally just been together earlier, and my heart was fluttering like I hadn't seen him in forever.

I couldn't stop the smile tugging at my lips even as I dismissed him. "Boy please, ain't no dick good enough to make me fuck up my bag."

"You know what? You right. I won't fuck up your gig, but I'm definitely gone see 'bout that later," he promised, leaving me stuck as he gave me a quick peck and finally sat down next to me. A mixture of fear and excitement shot through my body in anticipation of the punishment he was going to put on my kitty later.

"Ugh, thank God! Wasn't nobody tryna see all that! Bad enough yo' brother done came and stole my girl. Both y'all just in here fuckin' up the vibe." Jazmin rolled her eyes at us over the rim of her glass before settling them on Yara and Saint who were tucked in a corner talking heatedly. I already knew without looking that Koi's ass was eating that shit up, but I wasn't trying to give her a laugh at Yara's expense.

"Don't be a hater, Jaz," I teased, sticking my tongue out at her, even as I nudged Psalm. "Can you go check on them?"

He stopped breaking down the weed he had on the table and looked over to where his brother and Yara stood disinterestedly. "They're cool. Yara would've already slapped his ass if she was really mad." I disagreed, especially since they'd already drawn the attention of a few people, but at the same time, I couldn't really say shit. Psalm knew them both way better than me, so if he said it was cool, then I'd just have to trust him because I damn sure wasn't going over there.

I settled back into my seat with a sigh but kept a watchful eye on them just in case. Psalm finally finished rolling up and lit his blunt while I vibed to the latest Meg Thee Stallion song that was playing. "Oooh, this my shit!" I rapped along and recorded myself, careful to keep him out of the frame, but it didn't take long for him to catch on to what I was doing. His eyebrows dipped as he leaned forward, coming into full view of the camera.

Flashing his teeth, he let out a thick cloud of smoke before kissing my bare shoulder.

"You bouta finally post a nigga on yo' shit and stop tryna hide me?" he said, surprising me once I'd ended the video. Psalm had made it clear that he didn't fuck with social media of any kind, so I'd always made sure to keep him out of any videos I made while we were together. Besides Malice recording us on that first date, we hadn't made anything official as far as social media was concerned. A lot of my followers had speculated, wanting to know who he was, but I'd dodged the questions every time, and considering that we hadn't been seen together since, they eventually died down. Him wanting to be posted on my page was a huge step and I couldn't help simpering as I asked.

"Really?"

"Yeah, really. Unless you got some niggas you tryna look single for." He looked me up and down, his eyelids already at half-mast from the weed.

"I meeeean, it's a few," I teased, rolling my eyes playfully. My smile grew wider when he tightened his grip around my waist and pulled me closer.

"Yeah, ayite, you better quit fuckin' playin' with me."

"Oooh, I know the nigga that ain't claimed me yet ain't jealous?" I feigned shock and clutched my invisible pearls, but his expression turned serious as he licked his lips.

"I thought that's what I did when I had you cummin' on my tongue that first night." He may as well have been talking directly to my pussy with how hard it thumped. A pleased expression crossed his face when he saw the effect that simple statement had on me because I'd glitched right then. "Right, stop fuckin' playin'. You been mine, so post the video so niggas know." He gave my thigh a squeeze and went back to smoking while I tried to get my pussy in check.

I did just what he told me, making a reel on Instagram with Usher's song "There Goes My Baby" playing. Almost immediately, my phone started blowing up with notifications congratulating me and asking who he was. I blacked out my screen instead of responding, though, and lifted my drink from the table. I wasn't about to start answering comments or I'd be on that post for the rest of the night.

Yara eventually came stomping back over with Saint trailing behind her. It was obvious that their conversation hadn't gone how he'd expected, but that didn't make him leave. In fact, while she and Jazmin finished drinking and dancing, he sat not too far away, watching her closely.

"You straight?" I heard Psalm ask him and figured now would be a good time to rejoin the girls, but he kept his arm locked around my waist. When I looked back to complain, he puckered his lips up for a kiss, and I cheesed goofily before obliging him. I felt corny as hell for how giddy he made me, but then I had to remind myself that I deserved to be happy. Malik had never been one to be overly affectionate in public, especially after he started gaining traction. That's when he stopped bringing me along altogether. Going from that type of relationship to being with someone like Psalm was such a stark difference that I still had a hard time accepting that it was real.

After he got his kiss, his arm slipped from around me so I could get up, and I grabbed my glass before strutting off. I made sure to put an extra switch in my hips, knowing that he was still watching even as he finished his conversation with Saint.

"Nahhhh, don't be tryna bring yo' ass over here now!" Yara laughed when I finally reached them.

"Ooooh, you got your nerve! Both y'all heffas tried it! Next time y'all invite me out, I'ma bring a nigga just in case," Jazmin shot before I could even defend myself.

"Don't put me in it, I'm nigga free!" Yara sent a pointed look my way. "Blame this one and Psalm for my hating ass baby daddy popping up." I could tell she was only partly kidding, so I took the opportunity to clear my name.

"Okay, okay, you got that, but in my defense, he really didn't say nothing about bringing Saint." I opted not to state the obvious, about how I didn't even like his ass and vice versa. Yara eyed me for a minute like she was trying to see if she believed me, before finally giving me a light tap on the arm.

"I'm just fucking with you girl. I already know how that fool is. He would've crashed this party with or without you and Psalm," she said, glaring in his direction briefly. I was glad she knew, but honestly, I felt bad for her. Saint had been out doing whatever the fuck he wanted, yet he couldn't even give Yara a night out with the girls. "It's cool, I need to take my ass home anyway. I got an early day tomorrow. Gotta get some work done before Angel drops off the kids."

"What! Naw friend, don't let him fuck up the vibe! That's exactly what he wants!"

"Yeah, don't leave."

Jazmin and I tried to convince her to stay, but her mind was made up. "It's okay y'all, it'll be other nights." She forced a smile even as I put on an overexaggerated pout.

"Well, I'm leaving too. I ain't tryna be no third wheel," Jazmin huffed, polishing off her drink. I knew that was coming. Jazmin and I were cool but not enough that she'd have stayed while her girl went home bored. If I wasn't obligated to stay I probably would've left too. They wasted no time gathering their things, and just like Yara had predicted, Saint was right behind her like a lost puppy.

I tried to enjoy myself for the next couple of hours, which was a little easier with Psalm there. He was always good company, and by the time we were actually leaving, I couldn't wait to get back to his house so he could make good on his threat. In fact, my pussy was anticipating it.

Psalm

I woke up and smirked seeing Amari still laid out snoring. I'd made good on my promise and had kept her up half the night fucking her fine ass into oblivion. She let out a little moan and shifted so that the sheets slipped, revealing more of her juicy ass, and my dick started coming alive. As bad as I wanted to dive in her walls again though, I knew she was definitely sore and tired, so I decided to let her make it for now. Instead, I kissed her forehead and snatched up my phone on my way to the bathroom. I frowned seeing that Unique had been blowing me up for most of the night as I emptied my bladder. We hadn't spoken since I left her house that day and although I felt guilty, I hadn't made an effort to reach out. I was sure Legend's anniversary had been the only reason she'd called me that last time anyway. It was her way to not let me forget that I was a piece of shit. Since that was out of the way, I really couldn't understand what she could want now, but I wasn't pressed to find out either.

Besides her, there were a few other calls and messages, but nothing I couldn't get back to later. I set my phone on the sink and flushed before starting the shower so I could get ready for the day. My stomach was already growling, and I knew in a minute Amari would be up ready to eat too. I brushed my teeth while I waited for the water to get hot, which didn't take long at all. A half hour later, I was fresh out the shower but Amari was still knocked out. I quietly pulled on a pair of joggers and stepped into my Nike slides before heading to the kitchen so I wouldn't wake her.

My fridge was fully stocked so I had everything I needed to make the omelets, bacon, and hash browns I had a taste for. I put on my playlist and got to work setting the items on the counter so I could prep it all. Once I had the bacon in the oven, I started to cut up some potatoes for the hash browns since I didn't like that frozen shit.

"Ooooh, a man that can cook and shirtless at that. Let me find out I hit the jackpot." I grinned, turning around to see Amari sitting at the center island in one of my wife beaters and a pair of boxers. Her wig was gone, and in its place were some Cleo braids that normally would've turned me off, but for some reason, on her, it made me want to bend her ass over and pull on them motherfuckers while giving her back shots.

I flexed as I turned to face her fully, making her eyes gleam. "Yo' man can do it all baby, I thought you knew that." I leaned over the island as far as I could for a kiss, and she happily met me the rest of the way. It was no doubt I fucked with her heavy because I wasn't even worried about whether she'd brushed her teeth yet or not, but when our lips connected, I was glad to know she had.

"Mmmm, you better live up to that promise too. As much as I love food, I'm gone be mad as hell if it's nasty," she teased against my lips.

"I don't make nasty shit. I *do* nasty shit, and when you done eating this good ass food, I'ma remind yo' ass of that." The smile on her face froze as I sucked her bottom lip in my mouth and tongued her down. She hungrily stretched her body over the island when I tried to pull away, and I was about to say fuck the food, but the front door chimed, letting me know somebody had just walked in. I groaned inwardly because it could've only been one of three people, and since Saint barely ever used his key and Yara hadn't called, I knew it was my OG. Amari jumped back, looking at me suspiciously before my mama's voice shouted over the music.

"Hello! Hellooooo!" Her heels clacked loudly against the marble floor as she grew closer and switched the surround sound off.

"We're in the kitchen, Ma."

"Ma?" Amari hissed with wide eyes. She instantly began fidgeting, first covering her head before realizing that she was braless and crossing her arms. Her nervousness was funny as hell, especially since there wasn't shit she could do about any of it without my mama seeing her. There was only one way into the kitchen and she was already approaching so it was too late.

"Oh, I'm right on time! You're cooking ba—" My mama's voice trailed off at the sight of Amari who still had her arms crossed tightly over her chest with an awkward smile on her face. She let her eyes travel over Amari from head to toe without saying a word, which made the shit even more uncomfortable. She finally nodded as she stepped farther inside. "Ohhhh, so that's why you're cooking. You're over here *entertaining*. Well, I'm Psalm's mama, Angel, and you are?" The way she switched up her tone had me looking at her crazy. She didn't sound shit like her usual self, and I knew it was because she was on some bullshit.

"I'm—ahem! My name's Amari."

"Amari? I can't say that I've heard about you. How long have you been seeing my son?"

"Ma, bro, what you on, and why you ain't call before you popped up?" I interjected, hoping that my frustration wasn't evident in my voice, but judging from the look on her face, she'd definitely noticed it.

With narrowed eyes, she moved further into the kitchen. "If you had checked your phone you'd know I did call yo' rude, black ass, you just didn't answer," she said pointedly, and I remembered seeing she had, but I'd forgotten by the time I got out the shower.

Smugly, she continued. "And I'm not on anything, I'm just making small talk."

I eyed her silently, trying to get a read on her. My OG could be mean as hell at times, and just from the buttery-sweet way she was asking questions, I knew she was on some other shit. "Small talk, huh?"

"Ain't that what I said?" She gave me a side eye before turning her attention back to Amari. "Sooo, Amari, how long have you two been talking? It must've been for a while for him to have you over, because Psalm doesn't really have women at his house, not since Un—"

"Aye, you trippin'!" I cut her off before she could speak on Unique. I hadn't even told Amari about her, and it would be fucked up if my mama was how she found out.

"What? I was just saying she must be special if she's already staying over and got you cooking for her." My mama feigned innocence as Amari burned a hole in the side of my face, but I purposefully kept my eyes on my mama. She'd come in and ruined the mood fast as hell, and I was ready for her ass to make her exit.

Sighing, I rested my hands on the island. "Ma, what's up, man? What you stop by for?" I asked before I could stop myself. Even without the bite, the question was for sure going to piss her off, and the way her neck snapped back, I knew I was right.

"Uh, excuse you! Don't get slapped, lil' boy! I came to check on you 'cause I haven't talked to you in a few days and—" The door chimed again and her eyes widened as another pair of heels echoed through the house.

"You brought somebody with you?" I quizzed, coming from around the counter, and she jumped in front of me.

"Before you start, Psalm, I didn't know you had company or else I wouldn't have—"

"Psalm! Mama Angel!" My jaw tightened when I recognized the voice shouting out to us as Unique. I glared down at my mama as she sucked her teeth and huffed like she had a reason to be annoyed.

"Are you for fuckin' real right now?" My face twisted into a scowl as Unique finally entered the kitchen dressed like a real housewife, which wasn't like her at all. She was just like me, opting to be casual in jeans and a t-shirt most of the time, only dressing it up when the occasion called for it. So, the skintight romper and red high heels she had on caught me by surprise. She even had her makeup done and wavy bundles hanging down her back.

She looked around the kitchen like a deer in headlights until her eyes landed on Amari, and hurt flashed across her face before it tightened in anger.

"Girl, didn't I tell yo' ass to wait in the car until I told you it was okay!" my mama snapped, pinching the bridge of her nose.

"I had to use the bathroom, but I'm glad I didn't wait. Who the fuck is this, Psalm?" She pointed, tears already filling her eyes, because just like my mama, she knew that I didn't bring just anybody to my crib. "And is that bacon I smell? Is you cookin' for this hoe!"

"Hoe? I got yo' hoe! Psalm, on my son, I don't know who this bitch is, but you better get her before I—"

"I'm his baby mama hoe, and on *our* son, I'll beat yo' ass all over this damn kitchen!" Unique was thirsty to say. That had Amari's head rearing back as she squinted at me.

"Baby mama?" she choked out, and I took a step toward her.

"Babe, I can explain—"

"Yes, baby mama!" Unique cut me off, and I'd had just about enough of her.

"Shut the fuck up, Unique!"

"No! Clearly you're out here denying me and our son! What the fuck do you gotta explain to her? She should've been known!" she screamed, and I jumped in her direction ready to choke the shit out of her, but my mama stepped between us.

"Psalm, I know you wasn't about to put yo' hands on this girl. You need to calm down."

"Then get her ass out my house! You should've never brought

her over here!" I fumed. I loved my mama, but I was definitely considering changing my locks if this the type of shit she was going to be doing with her keys. She was just complaining to me about Unique even calling her, and now she was bringing her to my house unannounced and without an explanation.

"Nigga, I ain't going nowhere!"

"Unique, if you don't shut up, I'ma let his crazy ass go. Now I brought you over here 'cause you told me you wanted to talk, and all you doin' is actin' a fool!" My mama had her hand on her hip as she checked her goofy ass, finally fed up herself with all of her theatrics.

"But—"

"You know what, I'll leave, 'cause obviously y'all got some shit y'all need to work out," Amari spoke up, trying to make her way around us, but I was right on her heels, ignoring Unique calling me.

"Where the fuck you think you goin'?" She was already in the hallway when I wrapped her up in a bear hug. I expected her to start fighting me off immediately, but she simply went rigid, breathing deeply in an attempt to calm herself down.

"I'm goin' home so you can talk to yo' *baby mama*," she said, putting extra emphasis on baby mama.

"Baby, you ain't gotta go nowhere. I ain't got shit to talk to her ass about. Come on now, we were having a good morning. Don't let her fuck it up." I buried my face in her neck, kissing her gently as I gave her body a little squeeze. My affection had the opposite effect though, because she snorted and tried to snatch away, but I still kept a firm grip on her.

"Yeah, we were until yo' baby mama that I didn't know shit about popped up! Are you still fuckin' her? Fuck am I talkin' about, of course you are! That's the only reason she'd be comin' in here doin' all that!" Her voice hardened as she spoke, making herself more upset with the reach she'd just made.

"Ain't nobody fuckin' that girl! I don't know why she's even here and you know that. I was just as caught off guard as you when she came in here!" I was beginning to get irritated. My mama bringing Unique definitely looked bad, and it was even worse that I hadn't mentioned having a baby mama to begin with, but she wasn't even trying to give me a chance to explain before she was jumping to conclusions. I thought our biggest issue was going to be me not telling her, but she had added a whole secret relationship that didn't exist outside of her mind.

"So why didn't you tell me about her? You've known about my baby daddy since day one, probably not who he is but you at least knew I had one. All the times we talked and you couldn't tell me about her and your son? That shit seems funny as fuck to me. Let me find out you and Saint are really more alike than you let on. My dumb ass thought I got the good brother and you just turned out to be the better liar." She tried to wiggle away, and this time, I released her because she was really blowing the fuck out of me. The second she was free, she damn near ran to the stairs but I was right behind her.

"You know damn well I ain't never lied to you! I ain't never say shit to you about Unique 'cause there ain't shit to tell! We been broke up and you startin' to look goofy as hell for even letting her ass come in here and fuck our shit up!" I spoke to her back as she reached the landing, but that insult had her whipping around quickly.

"Fuck you, Psalm! If I look goofy it's 'cause yo' ass left me in the dark, but don't even worry about it! I'll take my *goofy ass* home so y'all can work out whatever the fuck you got goin' on!" Once again, she stormed away. When she realized I wasn't following her, she slammed my bedroom door behind her. As bad as I wanted to get this shit sorted out, I didn't want to continue giving my mama and Unique a show, so I went to get them out of the house. They'd both made their way into the hall, trying miserably to eavesdrop, and my jaw tightened at the smile on Unique's face. Of course, she was happy that she'd come in and started some shit.

I snatched her up by the arm and ushered her to the door as

she stuttered, and my mama followed behind trying to talk, but I wasn't trying to hear that shit. She'd shown the fuck out even bringing Unique here, and once I got shit right with Amari, I was going to tell her ass about herself. Once they were both on the other side of the threshold, I slammed the door shut and locked it like that could do something to stop my OG from coming back. I wasn't worried about that though. I was too busy trying to get back to Amari, who must've been related to Peter Parker with how fast she was already dressed in some of my clothes and making her way down the stairs. She'd put her wig back on and had her dress and heels from the night before tucked under her arm. As soon as she saw me at the bottom of the stairs, her nose turned up and she rolled her eyes but continued to come down.

"So you really not gone hear me out?" I moved to block her path and she went to the other side of the staircase.

"Nope."

"Bro, I ain't bouta kiss yo' ass, for real. I told you I don't fuck with her and you actin' like you caught a muthafucka doing something!"

"No, I'm acting like yo' ass is a liar, but if that's how you feel, I don't got no control over that." I stared at her ass for a minute, too blown to speak. How we'd gone from me making her breakfast and kissing to her leaving pissed off at me was beyond me, but I was serious when I said I wasn't about to kiss her ass. Clearly that nigga Malice had fucked her up something serious for how crazy she was acting.

"You got that," I told her, moving out the way so she could pass. She hesitated for a brief second, probably rethinking this whole shit, but stubbornness won and she left without looking back. Beyond irritated and in need of a blunt, I headed back to the kitchen and grew even more angry at the stench of burnt ass bacon. Tossing that shit, I cut the oven off and headed back upstairs to roll up and make an online order from somewhere.

YARA

I tried to control the anger I felt building up inside of me as I watched the video of me and Saint in the club. Even without the audio it was obvious we were arguing and everybody in the comments were speculating on why. It was the typical Shaderoom shit, that I often commented on and was right there along with everybody else talking about, but since it was my situation I was irritated as hell. I'd kept me and Saint's issues out of the public eye to the best of my ability, knowing that my fans would want an explanation, and I hadn't been quite ready for that, mostly because I wasn't sure if I was going to give him another chance or not. Shit, I still wasn't ready, but it was too late. This was one of the main reasons I hated being in the public eye. Nothing was private and anything that people thought they knew, they spoke on it no matter if it was accurate or not.

"You okay, friend?" Jazmin asked from beside me. She'd been here when my phone started going off with all of the notifications from people tagging me.

"Hell no, these muthafuckas in the comments goin' in. Talkin' shit about how they knew our relationship was too good to be true, and not to mention the random hoes trying to claim they fucked with him before—"

"Hold up bitch, who!" she cut me off and snatched my phone out my hand. For every comment she read that she didn't like, she'd let out a grunt and talk shit until she couldn't take it anymore and finally handed it back. I watched as she pulled the post up on her phone with narrowed eyes.

"Don't say nothin' crazy to them people, girl." I went to stop her and she held her phone just out of reach, thumb still moving furiously across the screen.

"Fuck these bitches! They gone let social media get them fucked up! You might not be able to say shit 'cause of yo' image, but I don't give a damn about mine!"

My phone rang, distracting me momentarily, and when I saw that it was Amari I took my time answering. It wasn't that I was mad at her, but I was definitely embarrassed. Saint had already shown his ass the night before in front of her and now the shit was all over the internet, so the world could see our disfunction. I ended up answering right before it went to voicemail and sighed once she came on the line.

"Oh my god, girl! Are you okay? I just saw that shit this afternoon. I can't believe somebody posted some shit like that!" she fumed, and I could hear her slippers sliding across the floor, letting me know she was pacing her apartment.

"I'm fine," I lied. "Just irritated that so many people got so much shit to say from a thirty-second clip." Despite the lie, I couldn't keep the bitterness out of my voice. I was usually cool about receiving hate from random strangers, it came with the territory, but this seemed different. For one, it wasn't just someone finding a reason to hate on me like what I normally experienced, and for two, they actually had something to talk about this time.

"Yeah, and if I gotta sit here responding to all their asses, I will! They better hope I don't find out who recorded it!" Jazmin still had her eyes glued to her phone as she talked shit, and I couldn't help laughing. The odds of her finding out exactly who'd been recording me in that packed ass club were slim, but if it made her feel better, I'd let her have it.

"That's Jazmin?"

"Yeah, she stayed over after we left the club last night. She's in here arguing with muthafuckas under the post and pissin' herself off." I chuckled, and Amari did too, despite the fact that wasn't shit funny about this situation.

"As she should, hell, I'm bouta get on there and do the same thing 'cause they're trippin'. Have you talked to Saint?" she wanted to know, and I grew quiet. The truth was that after we left the club his stupid ass completely left me alone and went on about his business. Basically, all he wanted to do was ruin my night, and he certainly had. Even worse, he'd ruined my day now too. Hell, my whole week was about to be fucked up at least until the next big story came across people's timeline.

I shook my head like she could see me and sighed heavily. "No, I haven't talked to his stupid ass yet, but I don't even want to. This shit is all his fault anyway, trying to come fucking with me, and now look. We're all over the blogs getting our relationship dissected." I really wanted to slap the fuck out of him and I couldn't wait until I could.

"It'll be okay, this shit is gonna blow over and folks won't even remember it happened once they find the next celebrity perv or conspiracy theory," she muttered, and I knew she was right, but that didn't stop me from being annoyed at the situation.

"Yeah, let's just hope that happens sooner rather than later. I need to make some type of statement, I just don't know what to say yet. You wanna come over and day drink while I figure that shit out?" My kids were down for a nap and likely wouldn't be up for another hour or so, and while they were asleep I was going to get my mind right.

"Hell yeah, I absolutely need some type of alcohol with the way my day's going." She sighed heavily and my forehead creased. I wasn't so deep into my own shit that I couldn't notice when somebody else was going through it.

"You okay, girl?"

"Not really, but it's nothing compared to what you got going on, so let me just call my mama right quick and then I'll be on my way."

"Okay, see you then." We hung up and I went to start making our drinks while Jazmin talked shit. It wasn't long before Amari rang the bell, and I handed her a glass as I answered the door.

"Oooh, just what I needed!" she gushed, happily taking a sip. "This is good! What is it?"

"Something I found on Facebook." I shrugged as I led her back toward the kitchen where we'd been sitting. Jazmin's glass was already empty, and she pushed it toward me with her eyes still glued to her phone. She'd been at it nonstop defending my honor, and I couldn't lie, some of the shit she was saying was funny as hell. I was glad Amari was finally there though, because I was struggling to get through what I was going to say. She was clearly much more levelheaded than Jazmin, and I needed that or else I'd be cursing out my own fans.

"I swear these bitches don't get tired. They must don't have a damn job to be sitting on Instagram all day!" Jazmin huffed as I refilled her glass and slid it over to her.

"How you gonna talk shit and you been doing the same thing?" I gave her a pointed look and she snorted, taking a sip of her drink before replying.

"I got a job, hoe, but right now, my job is putting these hoes in their place. They got you fucked up, friend, and since you gotta be the friendly influencer, I'll be the mean best friend that'll fuck a bitch up." She shrugged. "Girl, what's wrong with you? You look a mess!" Her eyes finally landed on Amari and widened in surprise. I hadn't mentioned to her that Amari was going through her own shit, and I damn sure wasn't rude enough to point out how she looked. I'd noticed the second I opened the door how puffy her face and eyes were. She looked like she'd been crying for hours, but I wouldn't tell her that.

I tried to discreetly pinch that bitch's arm and she jerked away with a yelp. "Damn bitch!"

"Stop being an asshole, Jaz," I hissed, forcing a smile on when I turned back to Amari, but she shrugged it off.

"It's okay, I know I look crazy."

"Yeah, but why? You should've been waking up thoroughly fucked and refreshed with the way you and Psalm were all over each other." Even I was confused about what could've happened between last night and now. When we'd left them at the club everything seemed okay, but I was preoccupied with Saint ass.

She looked off with her glass to her lips. "Everything was fine until Psalm's baby mama popped up with his mama while he was making me breakfast."

"His mean ass cooks?" Jazmin's extra ass gasped, and my nose turned up at the mention of Unique. Angel had been at my house and hadn't mentioned shit about going to Psalm's house or that she was with her son's estranged baby mama.

"What the fuck was Unique and Angel even doing together?"

"Shit, the better question is why the fuck didn't he tell me had a kid? We talk a lot and he ain't never mentioned nothing about his son or his baby mama, and why the hell did his mama bring her ass to his house? I was already looking a mess without my wig on and half naked, then she walks in looking like an Instagram model with his mama." Amari sighed and shook her head before her gaze shifted to me. "Girl, why didn't you tell me about her?"

She didn't sound like she was mad or accusing me of being sneaky, but I still felt bad that she'd walked into the situation with Psalm blindly. I knew firsthand how hard it had been for him when they'd lost Legend, and Unique's unwillingness to let go only made shit worse, which was why they didn't end up working out. After their breakup, she had slowly slithered into obscurity, which gave Psalm a chance to move on from his past. Honestly, I hadn't expected him to bring up Unique and Legend for a long time if at all, and Angel forcing his hand by bringing her around with Amari there was fucked up.

I ran my tongue along my teeth as I tried to find a way to explain it to her without seeming like we'd all been in on some big conspiracy. Obviously, he hadn't explained anything to her if she thought he had a kid around, and I knew he'd probably shut down on her instead of explaining like he should've. "Honestly, it wasn't my place to tell you, plus I thought once he trusted you enough, he'd tell you himself. I guess Angel just beat him to it, but I promise it's not what you think," I said slowly, and her brows dipped.

"That's what he said... What am I not getting that you all seem to know but won't say?"

"Don't look at me." Jazmin threw her hands up and looked my way. "Just put this girl out her misery and tell her what happened." She sucked her teeth in annoyance and I gave her ass a dirty look.

"Jaz!"

"Oh fuck it, I'll tell her—"

"Fine! Fine...*I'll* do it," I cut her off before she could go any further. Turning to Amari, I noted the frustration on her face before speaking. "Remember when I told you that Psalm had been going through it for the last few years? Well, that's because he and Unique's son Legend was stillborn, and that, among other things, ruined their relationship. It was like five years ago, but they just broke up last year, so I guess it's still kind of fresh." My voice trailed off as realization came over Amari's face.

"Why wouldn't he have just told me that? He let me accuse him of still fucking with her and some more shit," she groaned, dropping her head in her hand, and I shrugged.

"Psalm doesn't talk about it, not to anybody, not even Saint. He threw himself into his music, and everybody sort of just let him, thinking that at some point, he'd come out of the funk he was in. When he met you was the first time I've seen him be carefree in years, and I wasn't about to be the reason he went back to that shit. If you had seen him, you'd understand." I couldn't help shuddering at the memory of Psalm's depressive state. She probably thought his mean streak was the worst of it, but him being sad all the time was truly much harder to deal with.

"Ughhh, I gotta go." She rolled her eyes before finishing off her drink.

"I'd probably give him a minute to cool off before trying to talk to him," I suggested with a nod. Legend and Unique were sore spots for him, and I knew him well enough to know that he was probably in a fucked-up mood and would be for a while. Shit, he was probably pissed off at Angel too for even bringing her over there with her messy ass.

"Yeah, you might as well sit down and finish drinking and wait until tomorrow or some shit to go back groveling," Jazmin added, and I mugged her blunt ass. She was definitely the wrong friend to talk to about any man problems, and she was proving why the longer that we discussed this shit.

"Here, I'll make you another one." I grabbed her glass, feeling like I needed another one of my own. Now that only half of Amari's problems were solved, I still had to handle my shit. It didn't take long for me to mix up another drink for us both, and I cut on my Summer Walker playlist.

"Look at y'all bitches going through it." Jazmin shook her head after a few minutes, and I shot her a look. "Don't look at me like that, it's true. This is exactly the reason why I don't got a man, 'cause all they do is give you headaches."

"I don't have a man, I got a baby daddy," I quickly pointed out, but she side eyed me.

"Bitch, please! We all know you're getting back with Saint. He's your endgame and ain't nothing wrong with that, you just gotta make sure you put the fear of God in him so he won't fuck up again." Suddenly, her eyes gleamed. "Why don't you go out with that nigga from the grocery store?" she suggested, nodding, and I regretted even telling her ass about that. I could feel Amari staring a hole in my face, but I chose to ignore her.

"Uh, first of all, I'm already dealing with a crisis. Going on a date would only make that shit worse, and besides, I don't even have his number anymore," I lied. I absolutely had his number still tucked away in the bottom of my purse. Of course, I had no intention of using it, but it was nice to look at and know that I could give Saint a taste of his own medicine if I wanted to. From the look on Jaz's face, she didn't believe me, but that was my story and I was sticking to it.

"What nigga from the grocery store? You got a number and I'm just now finding out about it? I need some details." Amari sounded far more excited than I expected, but then again, her and Saint didn't get along, and after seeing how down I'd been, she was probably all too happy for me to focus on another man. Sliding off my stool, I snatched up me and Jazmin's glasses because we were both done. The liquor was causing her to have even looser lips than normal and it was distracting me from the task at hand.

"Hey, I wasn't finished with that!" she shrieked but didn't make an attempt to move.

I poured the rest of her drink down the drain and set her glass in the sink. "Now you are, big mouth!" I stuck my tongue out at her and she pouted childishly.

"So you really not gone tell me about the mystery man?" Amari huffed, and I rolled my eyes.

"It's nothing to tell. He saw me, he tried to shoot his shot, and after I shot him down, he insisted that I take his business card. That's it, but I'm not even thinking about calling him, especially when me and my baby daddy are getting dragged all across social media. The last thing I need to do is be caught with another nigga. That's really gone have people turning on me like I'm the problem." I was already shaking my head at the thought. I'd be pissed if I ended up getting backlash when Saint was really the one in the wrong and people just didn't know it.

"Well then, just have him come over here," Jazmin's thirsty ass tossed out there, and my mouth fell open.

"Now you know it would be dead ass wrong if I brought another nigga in our house."

"Shit, then go to his, but at least do something! Saint gets away with murder fucking with you! You think all these bitches in the comments are lying?" She went back to the comment section of the original post and started scrolling through as I struggled to come up with a good argument.

"Should I? Bitches lie all the time and we all know that clout is a hell of a drug." I sounded crazy as hell even as I said it, and she pursed her lips and slid her phone over to me.

"Well, at least we know everybody ain't lying," she grumbled as my eyes landed on the latest Shaderoom post. It was a screenshot of text messages between what was supposed to be Saint and a bitch that had blacked out her name. In it, they were talking about him fucking her, and I swear it was like my soul left my body. Knowing that a nigga had cheated on you and seeing that shit in the flesh were two different things, and this actually hurt worse than him telling me from his own mouth. Not only had he cheated, but the bitch wasn't even discreet enough not to jump on the bandwagon and make the shit public. Before I could stop myself, I was grabbing the bottle of tequila that I'd been using to make our drinks and put it straight to my lips. My day had officially gone from bad to worse real quick.

Koi

I watched Yara crashing out online and couldn't stop myself from smiling. When I'd first sent the video of her and Saint arguing, I hadn't expected for it to blow up the way it had. Couples fought all the time, especially celebrity couples. At the most, I figured people would speculate and it would just put a negative spotlight on her for a few days, but when I saw so many people talking shit about her and Saint, I figured I'd add a little razzle dazzle to it by posting some messages between me and Saint.

She literally hadn't even got the chance to address her adoring followers before I sent that shit over, not even caring about the way people would flock to her. I knew she'd lose her shit knowing that it was more than speculation. She along with a few others assumed that Saint was a cheating ass nigga, but having proof was something totally different. Plus, I had to show up the hoes in the comments section that were straight lying on his name. I knew for a fact he wouldn't have looked in half of their directions, and the other half weren't even on his level. The selfish part of me wanted to let it be known that I was the only one with actual proof of having been with him, but I wasn't stupid enough to reveal myself. The way the girls would turn on me, calling me everything from a homewrecker to a thirsty stalker and I'd fuck around and lose everything that I'd gained since becoming an it girl.

Unable to contain myself, I jumped in her live and liked it, smiling as I did. Yara looked a hot ass mess. Her hair was all over her head and she had makeup smeared all over her face from crying for the last few days. I read a few of the encouraging comments and scoffed at how lame everybody sounded. The more they tried to make her feel better the harder she cried, but she quickly got herself together when SJ ran his big-headed ass in the room. I could admit that he looked just like his daddy, but something about his face still reminded me of Yara's ass, which put me in a nasty mood every time I saw him. She wiped her face but still looked a mess as she tried to lie to him about why she was crying.

"Koi, I know you heard this girl in here crying!" My mama's voice snatched me from the glee I was seeing on screen, and I looked at her with my face balled up, pissed that she'd entered my house without knocking. Honestly, I hadn't heard her little ass crying, but I was glad that she couldn't get out of her room on her own.

"Actually, I didn't, but since you're already in here you might as well get her yourself." We stared each other down for a few seconds before I put my attention back on my phone, done with the conversation and her ass. I could still feel her eyes on me, but eventually, she carried her ass on so I could focus back on what Yara's stupid ass was saying.

"Naw, 'cause for real, fuck Saint and whatever little scary ass hoe he messing with! Somebody come tell her ass to get her nigga 'cause he still on my phone begging! She can have him, 'cause it's plenty of niggas that I can choose from!" she ranted, and I assumed that while I was talking to my mama, SJ had finally left the room again for her to be talking so reckless. She was better than me, because I would've let my baby know it was her daddy's fault I was crying. I never allowed a nigga to get the last laugh on me! If I couldn't directly inflict pain then I'd make the thing he cared about most hate his ass and then take him for everything he was worth in child support court, but that's where I differed from these other weak ass bitches like Yara and Amari. They let love cloud their judgement and all I saw was the dollar signs. Then again, the lengths I was going to, to get Saint's attention had far surpassed what he had in his wallet, but at this point, I was convinced it had more to do with me one-upping his baby mama. Probably didn't even have shit to do with him, I just didn't want to see Yara win, and she wouldn't if I had anything to do with it.

The little message she'd sent didn't do shit but make me want to stick it to her even more, and I closed out of her live so I could find some more of me and Saint's texts to taunt her with. I slowly scrolled through our thread until I came up on one where he mentioned how bad he wanted to see me and that she'd be too busy recording to even notice he was gone. After blacking out my name, I sent it to my plug at the Shaderoom, growing excited at the frenzy it would send the girls into. They were so thirsty for the scoop that they posted that shit right away, and I smiled as the likes and comments started rolling in. I didn't even let another second go by before going back to Yara's live, and just like I thought, they were already telling her about another series of texts that had been posted.

"Koi, this girl is burning up! How long has she been like this!" My mama stood in the doorway with a red-faced Blaze on her hip. She had her head resting on my mama's shoulder and was looking at me with watery eyes and a snotty nose. She was definitely sick, even I could see that, which had me ready to put them both out. I hated catching colds, and I'd learned the hard way that when she was sick I could and would catch whatever it was that she had.

I sat up from my spot on the bed and frowned. "I don't know, Ma. She was fine when Dola brought her back, but she must've got that shit from his house. Let me call his stupid ass so he can come right back and get her 'cause I'm not bouta get sick." My irritation was already high because they'd interrupted me, but now her dumb ass daddy had possibly put me at risk of getting a cold, so I was doubly pissed.

"What you want, Koi? I'm kind of busy," he answered and had the nerve to sound annoyed, which only set me off more.

"Well, you better get unbusy, nigga! Why the fuck is Blaze sick as hell and running a damn fever? Where the fuck did you have my baby? 'Cause she was fine when I sent her to you," I fumed, rolling my eyes as my mama disappeared from the doorway and made a mental note to schedule someone to come and sanitize my house since she wanted to walk around with Blaze's sick ass.

"You sound stupid as fuck! Why would I have her anywhere that I thought would get her sick? What's her temperature and how long has she been having symptoms?" he quizzed, moving to a quieter location.

Sucking my teeth, I pressed the phone between my ear and shoulder so I could log into my social media on my iPad. I knew Yara had to be foaming at the mouth by now, and he was keeping me on the phone asking me about symptoms like I was a doctor or something. "Nigga, I don't know, maybe 'cause you like irritating me like you're doing right now! My mama got her in the other room, but from what I can tell she just has a fever and a runny nose. I'm not bouta go check though, you know I get sick really easy." I went straight to Yara's page as soon as I was logged in and tried to find her live, but it had already ended a few minutes ago. I was still able to go watch the video though since she hadn't deleted it.

I vaguely heard Dola snort a laugh in my ear as I turned the volume up on Yara's video, but unfortunately, as soon as somebody mentioned the new text messages, she ended it. *Shit!* I had really wanted to see her reaction to them up close and personal.

"Koi! Did you hear what the fuck I just said!" Dola barked, damn near busting my ear drum.

"What, shit!" I tossed my iPad aside and tuned back in to the conversation. At this point, I just wanted to get him off my phone because he was getting on my nerves.

"I swear to God, I don't know how I got yo' sorry ass pregnant, bro. Tell yo' mama I'm on my way to get her, and you better hope I even bring her back to yo' stupid, unfit ass!" he spat, hanging up on me. Unfazed, I returned to Instagram to read some of the comments. The last thing I was worried about was Dola winning custody let alone even fighting for Blaze. He tried to pretend like he cared so much but he was just as happy to be free to live his life as I was when she was being cared for by someone else.

I didn't even bother telling my mama what he'd said. She'd know he was there to get her when he showed up. I was halfway through a shit ton of comments calling Yara stupid when he finally arrived, and I didn't move a muscle. Blaze and my mama at this point could give me twenty feet until they were cleared of whatever the fuck they had going on. It didn't take him any time to come and go, but once he did, my mama brought her ass to my doorway again, giving me what I guessed was a look of disapproval.

"Koi, what the fuck is wrong with you? Your baby is running a temperature of over one hundred degrees and you can't even come out to check on her!" She really had her nerve when she barely gave me any attention. Her ass was far from mother of the year, and we both knew that, which was why she was going so hard for Blaze. She must've thought that she could redeem herself by being a good grandma to my baby, but that shit did not cancel out the things I'd gone through as a child dealing with her, and I was going to make sure she didn't forget that shit.

"I guess like mother like daughter, huh? Don't act like you give that much of a fuck about me or Blaze, girl. If anything, you should be happy that I was able to give her a father that actually gives a fuck, unlike yo' ass." I barely spared her a second glance as I focused back on what I had been doing.

"Bitch, I will—"

"I wish you would try and touch me. I call the police over here, and yo' ass gone be sitting in lock up tryna find somebody to come bail you out." My lip curled as she stopped in her tracks, and if looks could kill, I'd be dead, but thankfully they didn't.

"You know what, you're not even worth my freedom. Plus, you got bigger shit to worry about anyway, because when Dola takes Blaze from you, yo' ass better hope you can still pay the rent since Amari's taking all your shine." Turning on her heels with a smirk, she disappeared out of sight and I waited until I heard the front door slam behind her before I let out an animalistic scream.

Psalm

Just like I always did when I had a lot on my mind, I locked myself in the studio and focused on my music. In a matter of days, I'd created a slew of beats and had written a few songs that were all ready to go to the highest bidder. I'd had to block Amari after that first day because she'd been calling nonstop trying to apologize, but I wasn't trying to hear that shit. She'd made her choice and I was going to let her have that. With my OG and Unique blocked too, my phone was unusually quiet, which helped me to put my all into the music I was creating. Eventually, I was going to unblock all of them, but I didn't know when that was going to be.

"Psalm, you got a visitor." The intercom went off and I cut the music down begrudgingly. I didn't have any sessions set up for the day so I didn't know who would've come looking for me, but they were about to get sent away.

"Tell em' I ain't here," I quipped dismissively, considering firing Layla for even bothering me with this shit when she knew I was working.

"She um—"

"She's not taking no for an answer, Mr. Savage." Hearing Free's voice instantly gave me pause. I'd cut her ass off years ago, so it was confusing as fuck what she could've been doing there. First Unique and now her. It was like I was stuck in that damn Christmas movie and all the girlfriends from Christmas past were visiting me or some shit. Going against my better judgment, I went ahead and told her to come on back. A few minutes later she knocked on the door and stuck her head in with a small smile. The years had been kind to her, because she damn sure looked just as good as I remembered. She'd cut her hair since our time together, and I had to admit that the pixie cut fit her well, showing off her pretty face and slender neck. I stood up to meet her as she stepped fully in the room and I got to see her entire body, including her round belly. My eyes focused in on it and I looked back up to see her smile faltering. Shaking off the surprise, I closed the distance between us and rigidly accepted the awkward hug she gave me without returning it.

"What's up, Free? I guess congratulations are in order." I tried to force a smile, knowing that it wouldn't quite reach my eyes. I was glad when she eventually let me go, sheepishly looking at the floor.

"Thank you. I know me dropping by is probably weird but..."

"Nah, it's cool," I lied as her words trailed off. "It's good to see you." I continued lying, hoping to cut down some of the tension in the room, and she giggled, taking a seat on the couch behind us.

"You don't have to lie, Psalm. Remember, I know you better than you think, and my popping up is probably more annoying than anything else, especially since I crashed your session," she pointed out, and I dropped back into my swivel chair with a chuckle of my own.

"You got me." I shrugged, scratching my head. "This shit is unexpected as fuck. What you doing out in my neck of the woods?" I was curious to know after not having seen her in years only for her to pop up damn near on the verge of giving birth in my studio. She swallowed hard and nervously twiddled her fingers as she searched the room. The Free I remember didn't normally exude so much nervous energy, and I wasn't sure what to make of it. It may have been because I'd threatened to kill her when I saw her ass again, but the fact that she even came back killed that theory. I tilted my head, waiting for her to speak, and her big brown eyes finally landed back on me.

"I, uh, I've been wondering that since I got back, and I guess it's because of this little girl here." She touched her belly affectionately, unable to stop herself from smiling. It was some shit I'd seen multiple pregnant women do, including Unique, and I used to think it was so cute, but at this moment it was making me uneasy. My forehead bunched in confusion and she let out another nervous laugh. "That probably didn't really answer your question. Um, I guess the simple answer is I came to apologize…again. Back when we were messing around, I was selfish, and because of that you lost time with Unique and your baby. All this time, I've been sorry about what I did, but the closer I get to Journey's arrival, the more I understand and I realize how important it is to right my wrongs." Her voice shook and her eyes became watery as her emotions took over. Just like every other pregnant woman I'd encountered, she was hormonal as hell, crying over shit that other people, especially myself, wouldn't give a damn about. I hadn't thought of Free in a long ass time and had long since stopped being mad at her. I was the one that was responsible for Unique. She was my baby mama and it was my son that I should've cared more about than getting a nut.

Before she could get herself even more worked up, I snatched up a stack of random napkins from some food I'd ordered and handed them to her. "It's cool, Free. Real shit, if I wasn't out chasing pussy, I would've been there and I accepted that shit a while ago. So you don't need to feel guilty or think some type of bad karma gone find you and your baby. We're good," I told her, hoping that it was enough to end this uncomfortable ass moment.

"Really? I-I don't know what to say." She dabbed at her eyes and sniffled while I tried to put on a reassuring look.

"You ain't gotta say shit, just go and safely deliver that baby and take care of her like I know you can." It made me itch just to be sitting there giving her ass a pep talk, but whatever got her out of there the fastest, I was willing to do. She popped up to her feet and I did the same, worried that she might fall over or some shit. Without warning, she threw her arms around my neck, pulling me into another hug that I didn't want, but this time I embraced her as well. I had to wonder if my sudden need to appease Free's ass was because of Amari's influence. No doubt, since meeting her, I hadn't been nearly as mean as I could've been. Normally, even after I'd acknowledged my role in what happened, I wouldn't have given a shit about making Free feel better, but here I was giving her a comforting hug when all I really wanted to do was put her ass out.

I was glad when she finally left after I declined her offer to treat me to lunch. Easing her mind was one thing, but I damn sure wasn't about to be caught out in public with her ass. Our situation was already weird enough. I spent the next few hours finishing up the beats I was working on and locked up so I could take my ass home. My phone went off in my pocket when I made it to my car, and I squinted when I saw Flex's name flashing on my screen.

Instead of ignoring his shit, I went ahead and answered. "Yoooo!" he brought his loud ass on the line, and I instantly regretted picking up.

"Nigga, fuck yo' ass always yellin' for? It's damn near midnight. You should be somewhere sleep!" I chastised with my face balled up as I climbed behind the wheel.

"Yo' ass getting old, muthafucka! It's Saturday, fuck would I be sleep for?" He laughed and I could hear somebody in the background cackling like a hyena. I already knew it was Vito's ass because that was the only nigga that hung around him often.

"Fuck you, and tell Vito to shut his bitch ass up!" My outburst only made them laugh harder, and I wasted no time hanging up on his ass. They were annoying as fuck already, but together they were a whole damn headache, and I was already in a fucked-up mood.

When he called right back, I ignored it, but he only called again like a damn stalker, and he must have finally realized I wasn't gone pick up because next he texted. My Bluetooth was connected, so it read his text out loud, and even Siri could hardly understand his broken ass sentences. What I could make out was him trying to convince me to come to the strip club with him, Saint, and Vito. I couldn't lie. It had been so long since I'd been inside a strip club. I considered it despite sending a text back that he could suck my dick. After the way the internet had been eating his ass up, I would've expected Saint to decline going to any club in an effort to get back in Yara's good graces. I'd seen the posts, and before he even told me, I knew it was Koi's ass sending in their text thread. I was surprised she hadn't exposed herself right along with Saint just for the clout alone; then again, I didn't think she was stupid enough to commit career suicide like that, considering how many people fucked with Yara. The next text from Flex was a video of a fucked-up Saint arguing with a stripper, and I knew I needed to go get his ass.

I pulled up at the Flamingo, and before I could get out, Saint came stumbling onto the sidewalk with Flex and Vito on either side of him. Them niggas thought the shit was funny as they struggled to get him to my car, and as soon as he sat his big ass down, the stench of Hennessey filled my nostrils.

"Nigga, damn, what the fuck yo' drunk ass do, bathe in that shit!"

He turned his red-rimmed eyes on me and pulled out a small pint from his pocket. "Shut yo' lil' ass up!" Grumbling, he reclined his seat all the way back and managed to take a drink from his bottle without spilling a drop.

"I'm gone let yo' goofy ass make it 'cause I know you gotta be fucked up behind what Koi did, but yo' ass ain't drinkin' shit else! Bad enough I gotta help you in the crib since you can't even walk on yo' own!" I snapped, mad that he'd allowed himself to go get so fucked up that he got carried out the club. He was too old for that shit no matter what he was going through.

Vito and Flex tried to talk to me, but I pulled off on their asses, not wanting to hear shit from them. They should've known better than anybody how bad it was for him to be in the club that fucked up. I had a mind to break both those niggas' contracts for being so stupid. I headed toward the apartment he'd finally rented, ignoring his drunk ass rambling beside me. In an effort to drown him out, I cut up the volume on the radio, but a second later he cut it right back down.

"Oh, I'm gone kill this bitch! Take me to the West side right now, bro!" He sat up, punching the dashboard, and I looked at his ass like he was out his mind. I could only assume the bitch he was trying to see was Koi, but I didn't know what more her slow ass could've done to him.

I was already shaking my head, still headed in the direction of his crib. "Hell naw, yo' ass ain't goin' nowhere but home, nigga. You ain't bouta get locked up on my watch—"

"Fuck that! I need to get over there now! This stupid hoe done posted our messages about the baby!"

Saint

Wifey: This is the last time you'll ever get to hurt me and I put that on my kids!

Yara had unblocked me just to send that message, and I'd been reading it over and over for the last twenty-four hours. Something about her wording let me know just how serious she was, and I didn't know what I was supposed to do. She was so pissed that she wasn't even trying to let me see my kids, and that wasn't even like her. No matter what, she'd never kept me away from our babies, but Koi's latest post had pushed her over the edge. Even when she'd gone on numerous rants in her lives, I'd never been concerned that I couldn't get her back. This shit was different though. Koi had really fucked us all up telling the world about that fucking abortion I'd made her get, and I was on the verge of putting out a hit on her ass. Psalm had convinced me to take my ass home the night I'd seen the post, and even though I'd listened to him, I still had plans to ruin that bitch, but first I needed to try and save my family.

I pulled up to our house and was both relieved to see Yara's car in the driveway and annoyed to see Jazmin's right behind it. Likely, if Jazmin was there then Amari's ass was too, and she was one of the last people I wanted to see. But considering that this was the first time in days that I would probably be able to see Yara, I was willing to deal with her presence. I smoothed out the t-shirt I was wearing and stepped out of my car before I had the chance to change my mind.

It was as if God was on my side because I'd barely made it up the steps when the front door swung open and a fully dressed up Yara stood there. My eyes traveled the length of her, taking in the tight little black dress she was wearing that hugged every curve Coco had given her and the open-toed red bottoms on her tiny feet. Her titties were sitting up something lovely, and every bit of skin that was exposed was oiled up and looking luscious. The smile that had been on her face when she'd first opened the door slipped fast as hell upon seeing me, and we both stood frozen just staring at each other until Amari appeared behind her. Fear covered her face and she tried to hurry back the way she'd come, but not before I noticed the difference in their attire. She had on regular ass clothes, nothing like what my baby mama was wearing, so any thought that they may have been going somewhere together was wiped away.

"You look...great ba—I mean Ya."

"What are you doin' here?" Her lips barely moved as she spoke, looking at me with so much hate that a nigga was ready to turn around.

"I, uh, I came to try and talk to you. I don't like being without you, and I know you're mad as fuck, but I don't think you like being without me either." I felt like Keith Sweat begging and shit, but it was really how I felt and I was hoping I was right when I said she felt the same way. That was until she busted out laughing.

"You don't know what I like Saint, 'cause if you did, you'd know I wouldn't like yo' ass comin' over here after I specifically told you to stay the fuck away from me."

"How the fuck else am I supposed to explain if you got me blocked on everything and won't even let me see the kids!" I was trying to control the anger erupting in my chest, but she was pissing me off. My fists clenched and I shoved them in my pockets. I didn't want her to try and run back in the house on me, so I needed to get myself under control, but seeing her like this was hard as fuck.

"Saint, please get the fuck on," she snorted with a shake of her head. "The very last thing you give a fuck about is these kids when you was out here putting us all at risk. I don't wanna hear that shit." She waved me off, and I rushed up the steps, this time unable to keep my outburst at bay.

"You a god damn lie! You know I love you more than anything! Did I fuck up and let some other bitch suck my dick every once in a while? Yeah, but I already told you that didn't mean shit to me, that was just pussy." As fucked up as it sounded, I figured the truth would set me free since wasn't shit else working, and that was the truth. Koi didn't mean shit to me and I needed Yara to know that.

Once again though, she was unmoved by the profession, planting her hands on her ample hips and tilting her head with a smirk that showed she didn't find shit funny. "Okay, so since you love us so much and that bitch was just pussy, tell me who she is." Her voice cracked at the end despite the hard front she was trying to put on, and I almost broke, but telling her about Koi was definitely going to ruin even the smallest chance that I could win her back. I licked my lips and looked off down the street, unable to stand the way her eyes were beginning to water as she waited for some shit that wasn't going to ever come.

"I...I can't do that Ya, baby. I—"

"Okay, so get the fuck on then. Go!" She pointed off into the distance as the tears she'd been holding back finally broke free. "Get yo' stupid ass outta here!" she continued to shout to the point that both Amari and Jazmin came running. This whole shit had went completely different than I'd imagined in my head.

"Yara, please, you don't really wanna know that shit, you just think you do."

That only seemed to set her off more, and the flurry of curse words had me taking a couple of steps back. "Fuck you, Saint! A whole fuckin' baby and you think you can just come over here and give me that bullshit ass apology and everything gone be all good! Fuck you! I hope you and that bitch die!" She looked like she was five seconds away from her head spinning like that bitch on the exorcist, and I was thankful that our neighbors were too far away to hear her or else the police would be on the way.

Jazmin and Amari held her back as she tried to come down to where I was standing. "Saint, just go. Damn!" Jazmin huffed, struggling to breathe. It was taking every bit of strength they had to hold her back, and as bad as I didn't want to accept defeat, I knew it wasn't going to be a win in this situation. Jaw clenched, I back peddled to my car, pissed and annoyed that we hadn't gotten shit resolved, but that wasn't going to stop me from trying again and again until I got her to see shit my way.

After leaving the house, I found myself in the bar, which was becoming a home away from home. I slid my glass back toward the bartender and she came switching over. She'd been low-key flirting with me since I'd gotten there, and I guess she figured the more drunk she got me, the easier it would be to convince me to fuck her. Little did she know, the last thing I needed was some pussy. Pussy had already gotten me into more shit than I could stomach recently, and adding another one to the fold would only make shit worse. She filled my glass up but didn't immediately walk away, and I raised a brow up in question.

"Do you need *anything* else? You know I'm getting off in like thirty." She tilted her head at me flirtatiously, making her long ponytail swing.

"Honestly shorty, this ain't the dick you want. I already got one crazy ass bitch damn near stalking me and a fiancée that will probably kill yo' ass. So yo' best bet is to punch out and forget you even saw me in this muthafucka," I told her, emptying my glass and motioning for another. Even with the warning, lust was still evident in her eyes as she poured the dark liquor for me. I waited until she topped me off and was about to try again before slamming a hand on the bar. "Bitch, get the fuck on! I was tryna let yo' thirsty ass down easy! Shit!"

Shock came over her face and she damn near dropped the bottle she was holding as she tried to back away. Everybody on my end of the bar was eyeing me like I was the one that was fucked up and not the bitch that sexually harassed me. I stared right back at their stupid asses and checked the time on my watch to see how long before the next bartender would get there, but after I swallowed my drink down, a heavy set of hands landed on my shoulders. I looked up to see two beefy ass members of security on either side of me looking like they were ready to rip me apart while the bartender looked on with a pleased smirk.

"You need to go," the one on my left said gruffly, pulling on my shirt.

"Aye man, what the fuck!" I struggled to get out of their grasp, but it was no use considering how big they were and how much I'd already had to drink. That didn't stop me from trying though. "Get the fuck off me!"

Every set of eyes landed on them carrying me out of the bar, and some even had their phones pulled out to record the shit. That had me cursing as I tried to fight them with no luck, and when we passed that stupid ass bartender, she made sure to stand just out of reach.

"That's why yo' *ex-fiancée* finally left yo' clown ass and is on a date with a real man!" That stupid ass bitch delivered that blow and then kicked me in my shin, making me growl. I was seeing red by the time they threw me out on the sidewalk as shorty's words replayed in my head. I didn't even know what I was more pissed off about. The fact that the bitch knew me the whole time, or the fact that Yara was on a fucking date. I'd threatened to kill Koi, but if I caught Yara with another nigga, I was definitely going to prison for murder.

Yara

I'd only been on this date for half an hour, and as hard as I tried to focus on what Isiah was saying, I could only think about the shit I had going on with Saint. It was clearly a bad idea to go through with the dinner, but seeing messages from Saint begging the next bitch to get rid of her baby just weeks after I'd had Coco was just too much. With Jazmin and Amari in my ear along with the mix of emotions I was feeling, I'd impulsively pulled out Isiah's number and agreed to go out with him that same night.

He was just as handsome as I remembered, maybe even more so with the perfectly tailored suit he was wearing and his freshly cut hair. Isiah was completely different than anything I was used to, and while I could admit that I liked him, I could also admit that I wasn't in the right head space to fully appreciate him. It was a shame too, because he seemed like such a great guy.

"Yara? You okay?" He waved his hand in front of my face with a sheepish chuckle.

"Oh gosh, I'm so sorry. I'm fine, my mind's just a little preoccupied," I admitted, instantly feeling bad for being that type of date and wasting his time. As cool as he was, I was fully expecting him to be pissed off or even annoyed at what could appear to be disinterest, but the relief covered his face and he lamely wiped imaginary sweat from his forehead.

"Okay good, for a second I was worried that my jokes weren't landing or worse," he leaned in and added lowly, "I was boring you, but since it's something else, I feel a lot better."

The tension I'd been feeling melted away as I giggled at his corny ass joke. "Well, making me laugh is a plus, so I'll give you a pass on maybe being just a little boring," I chided, lifting my wine glass with one hand and pinching my fingers together with the other.

"Ohhh, I see you got jokes, huh?"

Shrugging, I couldn't help but smile. "I do a lil' somethin' somethin'."

"You got that." He sipped his drink and nodded in approval. "So, how does an attractive, smart comedian like yourself end up single?" I hadn't been expecting him to ask me something so bluntly, and I damn near choked on my wine. There was no way I would tell him that the reason I didn't currently have a man was because the man I'd been engaged to and had children with was a big ass hoe that had embarrassed me all over the internet. "Oh, I'm sorry if that was too forward. Sometimes I put my foot in my mouth and—"

"No, no, it's okay. Um, whew." I blew out a puff of air and tried to find the right words that would explain my situation without giving too much away. Really, if he wanted to know, a simple Google search would give him the entire damn story in video format, but I didn't take Isiah as an influencer internet sleuth. That didn't stop me from worrying that he might stumble across that shit by accident. With the help of Amari and Jaz, I had tried to take down my live videos and anything I'd put up in my drunken rages, but there was still other people's think pieces. I sucked my lips into my mouth and blinked rapidly. "Well, I guess you could say that I haven't found the right person yet," I said, knowing the answer was generic as hell even as I said it, but even if he thought so too, he didn't point it out. Instead, he nodded like he was really into what I was saying.

"These days it's hard to find people that are ready for anything serious. Men and women alike are too caught up in living their lives and partying as much as they can. All too many of our peers are opting for the more—ahem, sexual connections." I bit back a chuckle at how uncomfortable he was saying that. He was definitely much different than what I was used to.

"I don't think that's totally true. I've met a lot of people our age that want the real thing," I disagreed. This type of conversation was so big online that my feed was constantly bombarded with sex war talk. Considering that I was recently engaged, I knew that there were some people out there that wanted real commitment.

He went to speak, but a commotion at the front of the restaurant stole our attention. We were nestled away in one of the private dining rooms, separated from everyone else by a mere curtain, but it blocked our view of the show my ratchet ass was itching to see. Isiah caught on immediately and a sneaky smile crept across his face.

"You wanna look, don't you?" I bashfully bit my lip and nodded. "Shit, me too," he said, reaching over to separate the curtains, and I did the same, but our location made it impossible to actually see what was going on. By now, shrieks and shocked gasps were ringing out as something came crashing down, and we shared a wide-eyed look. "I think they're making whoever it is leave," Isiah whispered like anybody could hear us, and a giggle bubbled up in my throat at how messy we were being.

"Naw, fuck that! YARA! YARA!" Hearing my name being called out by none other than Saint's stupid ass killed every bit of humor I felt. I snapped back up in my seat and dropped my head in my hands as he continued yelling my name like a damn fool.

"Did-did he just say Yara?" Isiah asked, voice full of confusion, and I nodded, too ashamed to lift my head. There was no mistaking my odd ass name. I couldn't believe his ass had found me, and it was really getting to the point that I was wondering if he had a damn tracker on me. "Umm, is that your kid's father?"

"Unfortunately...yes," I groaned lowly as the sounds of struggle grew louder. Cursing under my breath, I shot out from behind the curtain and raced past a restaurant full of people to the front, where the police had arrived and wrestled Saint to the ground. He lay on his stomach with a look of defeat on his face while an officer questioned the ragged-looking staff. The front of his shirt hung off his body, exposing his bare chest when they lifted him to his feet, and he narrowed his eyes upon seeing me.

"Yara." At that same moment, Isiah appeared at my side, standing so close I could feel his body, and I sighed as Saint looked between the two of us. His face instantly balled up, and he became irate again, struggling to get away from the police.

"This what the fuck you doin', Ya! You talked all that shit just so you could go on a date with this goofy ass nigga! On my soul, you got me fucked up!" he continued to yell as they dragged him away, and I stood there frozen. I could even feel Isiah trembling beside me with his scary ass, but I wasn't going to hold it against him considering that Saint was acting like a psycho.

"Um, do you—"

"Could you take me home please?" I didn't even wait for him to agree before walking back to our seats to retrieve my purse.

The ride to my house was silent and I was glad that he wasn't bombarding me with questions. He was probably too afraid to, but I was going back and forth between pity and irritation. It was crazy how he'd been able to do all his dirt and publicly embarrass me but felt like he had the right to be upset about a simple ass date. I really had a mind to bond his goofy ass out just to fuck him up, but I figured a night in jail would suit him much better. I hoped the whole night he was plagued with thoughts of Isiah getting the pussy and him being stuck there unable to stop it.

I was so deep into my fantasy of tormenting Saint that I didn't even realize we'd arrived at my house until Isiah called my name. "Yara, we're here." He touched my hand lightly.

"Oh, uh, thank you... and I'm really sorry about tonight. He really isn't like this. I guess he's taking the breakup kinda hard and if you don't wanna see me again, I'll understand." I'd barely finished, and he was scoffing.

"Why wouldn't I wanna see you again? His actions don't have any reflection on you. It might sound crazy, but I'm even more intrigued. You gotta be amazing to make a nigga act out of character like that," he joked, and despite the evening's craziness, I chuckled, glad to see that Saint hadn't driven him away with his antics.

"Well, I'm happy to hear that." I felt silly smiling the way I was, but it helped that he had the same expression on his face too.

We sat staring at each other for a few seconds before he finally seemed to realize how crazy we looked. "Oh, let me get your door." He rushed to get out, almost running around the front of the car to my side. I accepted the hand he held out to me and we took our time walking to my front door. "Soooo?"

"Sooo?" we said at the same time after I'd unlocked the door and we stood facing each other.

"I guess I'll call you." It came out as a question, but I nodded to try and calm his nerves, making him smile widely. Instead of coming toward me like I was expecting, he went to walk away, and I boldly snatched him back, surprising him with a kiss. His lips were just as soft as they looked, and his breath was minty, like he'd somehow managed to sneak a piece of gum when I wasn't paying attention. Moaning, I pressed against him, getting deeper into it before ducking across the threshold.

"I'll be waiting on that call." I grinned, slamming the door behind me and leaving him stunned. I'd deserved that kiss and I was glad I'd gotten it before I chickened out. It was weird kissing anybody besides Saint's ass, but I could see myself doing it again, and I couldn't wait until I got the chance to.

AMARI

I watched my phone ring with a call from Yara and sighed when it finally stopped. I'd been trying to avoid her ever since Koi started exposing her and Saint's texts. It was hard being around her knowing what I knew and seeing how much that shit was hurting her. She'd been spiraling and I knew a lot of it had to do with her not knowing who it was sending their texts to the blogs. It certainly didn't help that Saint was going out of his way not to tell her who he'd been cheating with. In her mind, he was protecting whoever it was when I was sure he was mostly protecting himself, but I couldn't tell her that without revealing my hand. I could really beat Koi's ass myself for all the drama she was causing.

I couldn't even escape that shit when I was working. If people weren't commenting under my videos asking about Yara, then I was hearing my clients gossiping or trying to fish for information. I always shut that shit down, but the fact that people felt entitled to a complete stranger's business was irritating as hell. Especially since Yara was the victim in all this but was catching hell like she'd done something wrong. Saint was getting Future level praise from niggas and Koi was completely left out of the fray. It was only right that her ass get the negative attention she deserved since she was the one that set this whole thing in motion.

"That must be a nigga or a bill collector callin', 'cause that's the only time a muthafucka don't be wanting to answer the phone," my client Symone cracked, and I chuckled despite knowing that it was neither. Since being in such high demand, I'd been able to pay up all of my bills, and the chances of Psalm calling me were less than likely. I'd realized after my calls kept going straight to voicemail that he'd blocked me, which meant that he wasn't trying to hear shit I had to say, and I kind of felt like I deserved it. Obviously, Malik had fucked me up more than I'd originally thought, and I hadn't taken enough time to heal before jumping into shit with Psalm. After our breakup, I'd thrown myself into survival mode, and now I was in hustle mode, so I still hadn't worked out my issues, but it kept my mind too busy to think about how I'd possibly fucked that up.

I spun Symone around so that she was facing me and started working on her baby hair. "Something like that," I said vaguely as I perfected her little swoops.

"I get it. I ignore my man's calls at least once a week just to let his mind wonder." She shrugged like what she said made any sense, but who was I to point that out?

Shaking my head, I continued to get her right. "You're crazy as hell girl, but you know what, that shit just might work." I couldn't help but to admit. Whether I could actually do it or not was an entirely different thing.

"I'm tellin' you, he be buggin' the fuck up like where you been? Why you ain't been answering my calls?" she mimicked a man's voice, making us both chuckle. Symone was one of my best clients. Just like me, she stayed out the way and never gossiped when she came to get her hair done. She was one of my loyal clients that had followed me from the salon when I'd finally decided to leave that toxic ass environment. I was working out of my home at the moment, but soon I'd be able to afford me a nice suite somewhere. I got giddy inside just thinking about it, and I stood back, smiling at my handiwork before putting a wig band on her so I could start on curling her hair.

In no time, I'd finished and she stood in the mirror snapping pictures of herself while I stood back like a proud mama. I let her finish and then had her stand in front of my grass mirror so I could take some of my own for my socials.

She was on her way to the door when Prince came running out, finally up from his nap and asking questions as usual. I put a stop to that with the mention of ice cream, and he rushed off to put his shoes on, giving me just a few minutes alone to prepare for the outing. Really, I didn't mind though, because I'd finally gotten a car of my own and I was in love with being able to get up and go. My little 2018 Ford Taurus was my second baby and I was so proud to have gotten it all by myself.

"Ready!" Prince returned, announcing himself loudly.

I eyed him from head to toe, trying to make sure nothing was out of place before we went out in public, and just as I'd expected, his shoes were on the wrong feet. Dropping down to his level with a squint, I asked, "Are you sure you're all ready?" My tone let him know that he'd forgotten something, and his little face balled up in confusion as he checked himself out. His inspection ended at his feet, and he looked up at me excitedly.

"Noooo! My shoes!"

"That's right, now get them on the right feet so we can go before all the ice cream melts," I told him, and he immediately sat down so he could switch them. I loved how happy he always was no matter what, and I prayed that as he grew up life didn't ever change him. Once he put his shoes on the right feet, we were off. Prince enjoyed our car rides just as much as I did, maybe even more. I'd gotten him a cute little Cars booster seat, a matching window shade, and activity station for his tablet and coloring books. I cut up his favorite song, and we vibed and sang along the entire half-hour trip to Legend Tasty House. It was one of the many places Psalm had introduced us to and we'd been addicted ever since. Now, whenever I even mentioned ice cream, this was what he expected.

I found a close parking spot, which ended up being half a block away, but Prince didn't even care. He babbled the entire way, completely unfazed by the journey since he knew there'd be ice cream at the end of it. Just like always, the place had more than a few customers, but my baby was just as patient as ever while we waited for our turn.

Once we reached the counter, Prince put in his order for Monkey Love while I got Matcha Queen. We found some seats, and I hurriedly set down napkins on the table, his lap, and the collar of his shirt for protection. As soon as I finished, he dug right in, getting that shit all over his face, the one place I hadn't been able to protect. I wiped it as much as I could before just saying fuck it and leaving it alone.

As usual, his mouth was going a mile a minute while I alternated between checking my emails, eating, and answering whatever questions I could catch. "Psalm!" My hand froze in midair hearing that nigga's name coming out of my baby's mouth. Like most kids, he'd asked about his new friend for a little bit before he eventually stopped, and I can't lie, I was happy when he did. It was already torture being ignored by him without Prince bringing his ass up every day, and now, after I'd finally gotten some peace, here he was again. I couldn't imagine what could make him randomly shout his name out of the blue. I tried to control the expression on my face when I turned to him, but his attention was elsewhere, and when I followed his gaze, there was the reason for his sudden remembrance in the flesh. He was all the way over by the register, but he'd heard Prince loud and clear, considering that his eyes were locked on us.

I took him in, irritated by how...unfazed he looked. My absence clearly hadn't had any effect on him, judging from his fresh haircut and well-put-together clothes. He looked like it was just an average Tuesday, and underneath my anger at the realization was...hurt. I thought I'd done a good job of functioning without him, and now I wasn't so sure.

By now, Prince was on his feet and everyone around was staring at him as he continued to yell Psalm's name. I was beginning to get pissed off by his lack of action when he finally smiled with a wave and stopped acting like an asshole to my baby. He finished paying for his ice cream and was on his way over, and my heart began pounding, but this time because of my nerves.

"Psalm! Hey, Psalm!" Prince bounced around as Psalm reached us.

"What's up, Young Prince!" Psalm held out his fist for a pound and his gaze flickered my way. He looked me over, showing not an ounce of emotion, and I died a little inside. It was one thing to know a nigga had you blocked, but it was something completely different for him to act like you didn't exist in person.

I was glad when Prince started talking excitedly, telling him all about our car and all the cool stuff he had in it. One thing I'd always liked about Psalm was his willingness to indulge my son; at least, that hadn't changed.

They chatted for a little while longer before Psalm finally shifted, looking uncomfortable, and I realized I hadn't offered him a seat despite him not speaking to me directly.

"You can sit down," I said awkwardly, holding my hand out toward the other side of the table.

"Uhh, I gotta get up outta here to be honest."

"Oh, okay, say goodbye Prince. We don't wanna hold Uncle Psalm up." I rolled my eyes over to my baby so I could avoid seeing the pity on Psalm's face. On cue, Prince started throwing a tantrum, not wanting him to go, and I groaned inwardly. "I guess it's time we leave too." I made an attempt at cleaning his face, but the melted ice cream had dried and even mixed with his tears. It wasn't trying to come off. Giving up, I collected our trash from the table so I could throw it away while actively ignoring Psalm who was still standing there. I grabbed ahold of Prince's hand, ready to get the hell away from him, but he chose to start walking at the same time, slipping to the other side so that he could hold Prince's other hand. I summed it up to him just wanting to stop all the crying, but it probably would've been easier if he'd just left again. Prince had gotten over his last disappearing act and he'd do it again. This shit here was probably just confusing him.

I resisted the urge to tell him he could go the entire way to my car. "Thanks, but I got it from here," I said, locking Prince in his seat, but when I backed up to close his door, Psalm was still standing there leaning up against my trunk.

"You did good, Amari," he spoke lowly, stalling me. It was the first thing he'd really said to me since coming to our table, and I was confused as fuck until he nodded toward the car.

I acknowledged it every day, proud of myself for the purchase and being able to get it myself. It was definitely a pretty car and ran like a dream. "Thanks, let me go ahead and get this boy home." This time when I went to walk away, I put a little bit more pep in my step and Psalm stayed in place up until I got behind the wheel and put the car in gear. His ass was confusing as hell because even after I pulled away from the curb, he stood there for a minute staring after my car.

Psalm

It took about five seconds after Amari pulled off for me to realize that I didn't want her to go. I'd been fighting not to contact her for a minute, and it figured that the one day I wasn't thinking about her ass, I ran into her. Seeing Prince had riddled me with guilt for just disappearing on him, and I could feel the judgment radiating off of Amari, which was why I had little to no words for her. It wasn't until I saw her about to leave that I began to feel that familiar ache in my chest. Before her car could disappear out of sight, I tossed my melting ice cream and climbed behind the wheel of mine.

In the time it took me to get out into traffic, I'd lost sight of her, but I knew a shortcut to her house. I hoped she was really headed there or else I'd be looking stupid as fuck. I beat every traffic law I could and managed to pull up to her building within half the time it would've normally taken. Putting the gear in park, I climbed out and checked my watch to see how long I had before she'd be pulling up. I didn't even know what I was going to say to her after the way shit had just gone down. That I was stupid. That I'd fucked up and had let her slip through my fingers over my pride. Shit, would any of that shit be enough? I didn't know how long I was out there contemplating before I saw her car creeping up the street.

She was so busy focusing on parking that she hadn't noticed me standing in the middle of the sidewalk, but by the time she came around to get Prince out, her eyes landed on me. We stared at each other silently for a few seconds before she finally found her voice. "What are you doin' here, Psalm?" her nose scrunched a little as she asked.

"I, uh," I stuttered, searching for the right words before realizing that there were none. Sighing, I took a step closer and drank her in. "I miss you. It took me about five seconds after you just left to figure that out. Shit, I knew the day you left my crib, I just let my pride get in the way. I didn't think I needed to explain myself to you, so I let you walk when all it would've took was a few minutes of being real with you. I am just saying that yes, Unique is my baby mama. Five years ago, I was laid up cheating on her when she went into labor and delivered our son with no heartbeat. We tried to make shit work after that, but she was stuck in the past, and we broke up like a year ago because of it. I really don't know how she got my OG to bring her over there that day, but I swear I wasn't on no funny shit with you. I would never do no shit to hurt you..." I trailed off, not knowing what else to say, and a long beat of silence passed between us. The shit was so long that I started to take my soft ass back to my car and peel out before I could embarrass myself anymore, but before I could take a full, step she stopped me.

"I know." She blinked rapidly, trying hard to stop her eyes from watering, and I closed the space between us. "I knew since the day after I left. Yara filled me in as much as she could without going too far into detail. I understood, though, but you had me blocked, so I couldn't apologize." She chuckled through her tears, and I brushed the few that had escaped from her cheeks before covering her mouth with mine.

"You don't got shit to be sorry for, baby," I told her with our lips still pressed together. We moaned into each other's mouths, our kiss growing deeper. "Fuck, I missed you so much."

"I missed you too," Amari whimpered, pressing against me, and if it wasn't for Prince yelling to catch our attention, I would've forgot shorty was even there. We separated, sharing a laugh at how carried away we'd gotten that fast as she wiped her lipstick from my lips. "Are you going to stay a while?"

"Hell yeah, I ain't going no fuckin' where till you tell me to. Shit, probably not even then." She laughed like I was telling a joke, but I was dead ass serious. I wasn't leaving Amari's side. Just the short amount of time that I'd been without her was enough to scare a nigga straight. Reaching over, I opened the door for her to get Prince out, and as soon as his little badass was in her arms, he was mugging me.

"Ewww! You kiss! "Only I kiss Mommy!" Grabbing Amari's face between his sticky hands, he gave her a kiss that I knew was full of slob and ice cream, but she let him with no objection.

I threw my hands up and took a step back, trying to keep the smile off my face. "My bad, man, you got it." He smiled widely like he knew what that shit meant, and Amari rolled her eyes. He held her tightly as she switched off and I followed behind her, eyes glued to her ass, thinking about how I was going to fuck her later.

Once we were upstairs, it seemed like Prince's animosity had melted away because he wiggled out of her arms and ran off, only to come back a second later with his cars. Amari cut on a cartoon for us, and we chilled in the living room, but even as I played with Prince, I couldn't keep my eyes off her. I should've felt some type of way about how fine she was looking, in the pale pink, two-piece set she had on. She wasn't even trying and she was killing bitches.

"Stop staring at me like that." She smirked, peeking at me from behind her phone.

"Like what?" My face matched hers as I eyed her breasts that were sitting up just right. I peeped her squeeze her thighs together, obviously feeling the same shit I was feeling.

"Like that." Her eyebrows shot up, and I chuckled.

"Yeah, I'ma chill before I have to sneak you up in the room or some shit," I told her, turning back to Prince who had been ramming his car into mine the whole time we'd been talking.

"Prince ain't goin' for none of that anyway, so you may as well practice your patience," she hummed, focusing back on her phone. I decided to let her make it because I knew as soon as Prince's ass went to bed, I was going to punish her pussy. I'd been backed up ever since she'd left, so I was definitely in need and so was she. Shaking off the thoughts I was having, I focused back on the game I was playing with Prince. I faintly heard her listening to some shit and figured she was on that damn TikTok app, but a second later, she let out a scream that had me and Prince jumping out of our skin.

"I'm gone kill that fuckin' bitch!" she shrieked, jumping to her feet as she cut the volume all the way up, and I heard Malice's voice. I'd paid little to no attention to his bitch ass since I'd knocked him out, even though he'd still been posting a bunch of lives still talking shit. Vito told me he'd just signed with Gangstas Inc., which was a much smaller record label than ours. I didn't give a fuck about that. It was the typical story of niggas who had an enemy in common teaming up, but Malice was just as weak as Geronimo, the head of the label, so anything either of them said didn't mean shit to me. I tuned back in to what Amari was saying but could only make out grumblings and growls as she paced the floor. Malice's voice was loud and clear though.

"Yeah, this goofy ass broad think she doin' something runnin' around with Psalm's bitch ass, but what she don't know is that I been fuckin' her girl Koi this whole time!" A chorus of oohs and ahhs sounded in his background while Amari watched, chest heaving. "Hey, why don't you tell yo' new friend Yara that this whole time the bitch that's been sending in those screenshots and fuckin' her baby daddy is Koi! You a phony ass bitch and I'm gone make sure I expose yo' ass today!"

To be continued...

Also by J. Dominique

Taken By A Rich Beast

Alone In Miami At 3AM 3

Alone In Miami At 3AM 2

Alone In Miami At 3Am

First Come Thugs, Then Come Marriage 4

First Come Thugs, Then Come Marriage 3

First Come Thugs, Then Come Marriage 2

First Come Thugs, Then Come Marriage

I Bought Every Dream He Sold Me 3

I Bought Every Dream He Sold Me 2

I Bought Every Dream He Sold Me

In Thug Love With A Chi-Town Millionaire 3

In Thug Love With A Chi-Town Millionaire 2

In Thug Love With A Chi-Town Millionaire

Every Savage Deserves A Hood Chick 2

Every Savage Deserves A Hood Chick

Chino And Chanelle

Chino And Chanelle 2

Chino And Chanelle 3

Giving My Heart To A Chi-Town Menace

Giving My Heart To A Chi-Town Menace: Real & Nova Story

Low Key Fallin' For A Savage

Low Key Fallin' For A Savage 2

Low Key Fallin' For A Savage 3

A Hood Love So Real

A Hood Love So Real 2

The Coldest Savage Stole My Heart

The Coldest Savage Stole My Heart 2

Made in the USA
Columbia, SC
02 April 2025